THE SWAMP MONSTER

THE HARDY BOYS® MYSTERY STORIES

THE SWAMP MONSTER

Franklin W. Dixon

WANDERER BOOKS

Published by Simon & Schuster, Inc., New York

Copyright © 1985 by Simon & Schuster, Inc.
All rights reserved
Including the right of reproduction
in whole or in part in any form
Published by Wanderer Books
A Division of Simon & Schuster, Inc.
Simon & Schuster Building
1230 Avenue of the Americas
New York, New York 10020

Manufactured in the United States of America
10 9 8 7 6 5 4 3 2 1

THE HARDY BOYS is a trademark of Simon & Schuster, Inc.
registered in the United States Patent and Trademark Office

WANDERER and colophon are registered trademarks of
Simon & Schuster, Inc.

Library of Congress Cataloging in Publication Data
Dixon, Franklin W.
The swamp monster

(The Hardy boys mystery stories ; 83)
Summary: The Hardy brothers go to Big Thicket, Texas,
to investigate attempts on the life of a naturalist
trying to preserve the area wildlife in the face of
threats from timber and oil interests.
1. Children's stories, American. [1. Mystery and
detective stories. 2. Wildlife conservation—Fiction]
I. Title. II. Series: Dixon, Franklin W. Hardy boys
mystery stories ; 83.
PZ7.D644Sw 1985   [Fic]   84-25682
ISBN 0-671-55054-3
ISBN 0-671-55048-9 (pbk.)

Contents

1 A Grizzly Warning

The Hardy boys were returning from an evening workout at the Bayport gym, when blond, seventeen-year old Joe pointed to a tan-colored car parked in front of their house.

"It seems we have company!" he said.

"I wonder who it is," his brother Frank added.

When they entered the house, Frank and Joe saw their father, a well-known private investigator, seated next to the fireplace with a tall, slender black man in a tweed jacket and corduroy slacks. Both men's faces were lined with concern.

"Hello, boys," Fenton Hardy greeted them. "Come on in. I'd like you to meet Professor

Martin Pierce. Martin's an old college friend of mine."

Frank and Joe shook hands with the visitor. They knew Professor Pierce was an internationally acclaimed naturalist, one who had fought long and hard for ecological causes. His face had appeared on the cover of a news magazine only a week before, after he had preserved a rich forest area in Montana.

"I've heard a great deal about you boys," Professor Pierce said, his serious expression momentarily replaced by a smile. "It seems Fenton has taught you his trade so well that now you're just as famous as he is."

Eighteen-year-old Frank grinned. "Not really," he said. "We're only amateurs, you know. Are you here on a social visit?"

"No," the professor replied, the smile gone. "I flew in from Texas because I need your help."

"Apparently someone's trying to kill Martin!" Mr. Hardy declared, coming right to the point.

"What!" Frank and Joe were shocked.

"There was more than one attempt, too," the professor added. "Two weeks ago, a bullet barely missed me out in the woods. The local sheriff thinks a careless hunter probably took me for a deer. But I know better than that. Four days later, a car tried to run me down on a logging road. My telephone wires have been cut, and I've received threatening letters."

Frank and Joe became instantly alert. Both boys had been well trained by Fenton Hardy, who had been an ace detective for the New York City Police Department before becoming a private investigator.

"Do you have any idea who might be behind all this, sir?" Frank asked, running a hand through his dark hair.

"I'm afraid I have a *very* good idea who's behind it," Pierce said dryly, gripping the arms of his chair. "I've been working in the Big Thicket area in southeast Texas. I don't know if you fellows are familiar with the place or not — it's beautiful country, covered with marshland and thick forests, and teeming with plant and animal life. We've got everything there from alligators and wild razorback hogs to rare orchids and trees nearly a thousand years old."

"I read a book about it not long ago," Joe nodded. "It's a naturalist's paradise, isn't it?"

"A good description," said Pierce. "And that's where I come in. I'm trying to help preserve the Thicket's plant and animal life. Timber and oil interests have threatened the ecological balance of the area for some time. The Thicket gets smaller every year, and there's a danger we could lose it all some day. I've been negotiating with Nelson Zeigler, president of the big Zeigco Corporation. He's a very pleasant, agreeable man," Pierce sighed. "I *thought* we'd found someone who really wanted to work with us instead of against us. Now, I'm not at all sure."

"Martin is almost convinced Zeigler is behind these attempts on his life," Mr. Hardy broke in. "Zeigler may be acting like a friend while stabbing Martin in the back, so to speak."

"I hate to say it," Pierce added grimly, "but Nelson Zeigler wants that oil and timber badly. It would be worth millions to the Zeigco Corporation."

"People's lives have been threatened for less than that," Joe said.

Fenton Hardy stood up and faced his sons. "I'd like the two of you to fly down to the Big Thicket with Professor Pierce. He's going back in the morning on a National Conservation Group jet. I have a case to wind up here, but I can join you in a few days."

Frank's eyes flashed at his brother. "We'll be glad to, Dad. Joe and I can get things started for you."

"I know you were planning on going camping with Chet Morton," Mr. Hardy said, frowning a bit. "Maybe you fellows can postpone that trip until later."

10

"Say, if you have a friend who'd like to come along, there's ample space in the plane," Professor Pierce offered. "I'd be glad to have him join us. Also, I've plenty of room at my house to put you all up. My wife's away on an archaeological dig, and I'd welcome the company."

"Great!" Joe grinned. "As long as you have lots of cheeseburgers and malts in the Big Thicket."

Frank caught Martin Pierce's puzzled expression and chuckled. "Eating is our friend's hobby," he explained. "Chet might even chase down one of those razorback hogs you were talking about and turn it into bacon!"

"He'd better take a good, hard look at one first," Pierce warned. "Frankly, I'd rather face an angry bear."

At that moment, Aunt Gertrude, Fenton Hardy's lanky unmarried sister, stuck her head into the room. "That's enough talking for now," she said firmly, brushing her hands on her apron. "I've got supper getting cold on the table."

"Better do what she says," Joe told Professor Pierce. "When Aunt Gertrude says now, she *means* now."

"*Hmmmmph!*" Aunt Gertrude gave him a steely-eyed look over the rims of her glasses. "I don't recall *you* missing many of my meals, Joe Hardy."

"He knows better," Frank laughed.

"By the way," Fenton Hardy said, "Martin tells me there's another mystery down there in the Thicket. It seems there's some kind of, ah, giant alligator on the loose in the swamps. A big devil, too—fifteen feet or more. It's terrorizing everyone in the area."

Both boys stared. "F-*fifteen* feet?" Joe asked dubiously. "Are you serious, professor?"

"Dead serious," Pierce said solemnly. "There aren't too many of 'em that size around, and this one's plenty smart. Every hunter and trapper in the Thicket has tried to catch him. So far, no one's even gotten close."

Before the boys could question Professor Pierce further, their friend Chet Morton opened the front door and walked in.

"I'm not surprised!" Aunt Gertrude said shortly. "That boy can smell food a mile away."

"Oh, were you folks getting ready to eat?" Chet said innocently.

"That's right," Frank said. "By the way, we were just talking about you. You're invited to join us on an expedition to the Big Thicket in Texas."

"I am?" Chet's eyes gleamed. "Great! When do we leave and what do I have to do?"

"We leave first thing in the morning," Joe said,

12

winking at his brother. "And *all* you have to do is track down a monstrous alligator that's running loose in the swamps."

Chet's jaw fell. "A—a *what!*" He swallowed and looked at the ceiling. "I just remembered something. I'm — going to be real busy this week."

"Busy doing what?" Joe asked.

"Oh, I almost forgot," Professor Pierce put in. "You boys will be in the Big Thicket during our annual Jayhawkers' and Rebels' celebration. It's really something to see. There'll be parades, rides, costumes, and a reenactment of a Civil War battle." He glanced at Chet. "Sure wish you weren't tied up, young man — hate to see you miss it. For two weeks there are booths along Main Street where pretty girls sell cotton candy, hot dogs, barbecued ribs, corn on the cob . . ."

Chet blinked. "I, uh—guess I might be able to get out of—whatever it was I was doing."

"We thought maybe you could," Joe laughed.

Pierce stopped abruptly on the way to the dining room and turned to Aunt Gertrude. "I just remembered," he told her. "I have a present for you out in the car. Wild orchids from the Big Thicket. I carried them with me on the plane."

"For me?" Aunt Gertrude clasped her hands and blushed. "Well, my goodness, professor!"

13

Pierce walked quickly into the hall and out the front door to his car. Moments later, a harsh cry of alarm reached the house. Joe, Frank and Mr. Hardy dashed out into the darkness, followed by Chet Morton and Aunt Gertrude.

"Martin, what is it—what's wrong?" Fenton Hardy asked. The former New York City detective had grabbed a flashlight in the hall, and now shone the beam directly at his friend.

Professor Pierce stood frozen beside the open door of the car. Frank glanced past him, and the hairs on the back of his neck rose.

"Look at that!" he exclaimed.

Crowded on the narrow back seat of Pierce's car was a three-foot-long alligator! Its thick, warty hide was the color of dead moss. Its sharp claws tore at the leather upholstery, and the heavy, powerful tail lashed out at the ceiling. Fenton Hardy's flashlight revealed eyes that burned like coals. The enormous jaws suddenly opened wide, displaying long rows of razor-edged teeth, as a terrible hissing noise came forth from the ugly creature's throat.

Frank stepped up and quickly slammed the car door shut. The alligator's jaws snapped shut, then opened again as it threw its snout angrily against the window.

"Leaping lizards!" Joe exclaimed. "You didn't bring *him* along, too, did you, professor?"

14

Pierce shook his head. "No. But there isn't a creature like that in this part of the country. Unless I miss my guess, this one is from the Big Thicket. *Somebody* brought it up here to scare me away from the work I'm doing in Texas—the same person, no doubt, who's been after me all along!"

2 *Flight into Danger*

The morning sun blazed over the horizon as three cars approached the south gate of the Bayport airfield. Police Chief Ezra Collig led the way, Fenton Hardy's car was in the middle, and Deputy Howard Kennedy followed behind. After the incident of the night before, Mr. Hardy was taking no chances.

"Whoever put that alligator in Professor Pierce's car meant business," he told Frank and Joe. "I'd be very surprised if the culprit wasn't still in this area."

"You boys watch yourselves now," Aunt Gertrude warned from the back seat. "You go looking for trouble, you'll find it sure enough!"

16

"Don't worry," Chet assured her. "I'll be keeping an eye on Frank and Joe."

"Now I *am* worried," Aunt Gertrude said shortly.

Joe grinned at her remark. His aunt was truly fond of Chet, but couldn't resist teasing him now and then. "Chet has helped us out on lots of cases," he told her. "He's turning into a pretty good detective."

"I am?" Chet beamed at the compliment. "Why didn't you say so before?"

"Because he knows you'd get a big head if he did," Frank chimed in. Then he turned to his father. "Dad, do you think whoever's after Professor Pierce might sabotage his plane? That would be a good way of making certain the professor didn't return to the Big Thicket."

"Heavens!" Aunt Gertrude's eyes opened wide with alarm. "What a terrible thought!"

"The possibility had occurred to me," Mr. Hardy said.

"We called my pilot and flight engineer last night," Professor Pierce put in. "They checked out the craft thoroughly, and the airfield security police promised to keep an eye on it."

"That's a relief!" Joe declared.

"Don't rest too easy," Fenton Hardy warned, his features clouded with concern. "Whoever is behind this isn't finished. He's certain to try again." He eased the car to a stop while up ahead Chief Collig slowed to ask the guard at the airport gate to let them through. Then the three cars sped quickly onto the flat expanse of the runway.

"That's it over there," Pierce pointed. "In front of the second hangar."

"Wow, what a beauty!" Chet exclaimed.

Mr. Hardy stopped in front of the sleek, twin-engined jet. It was painted a gleaming white, with sky-blue striping along the sides. As Chet removed his bag from the trunk, Pierce noticed him studying the emblem on the plane's tail, that of a white bird in flight, encircled in blue.

"It's the symbol of the National Conservation Group," he explained. "Do you recognize the bird?"

"No, I don't think so," Chet replied.

"It's a passenger pigeon," Pierce explained. "In the 19th century there were countless millions of them in this country. Sometimes they blackened the skies like clouds."

"I've heard about that," Frank said as he came up behind the two. "They're extinct now, aren't they?"

"Hunters killed them for food, and just for the sport of shooting them," said Pierce. "Our group adopted the bird as our symbol, to remind us of what can happen. When these birds were plentiful, no one ever dreamed they would disappear. Now, all we have left are stuffed specimens in museums."

"That's really what your cause in the Big Thicket is all about, isn't it?" Chet commented.

"That's it exactly," Pierce said. "Come on, we'd better be getting aboard. . . ."

Frank and Joe shook hands with their father, and thanked the graying, portly Chief Collig for his help. Aunt Gertrude hugged the boys and handed Chet a basket containing more fried chicken and potato salad than they could possibly eat.

In moments, the jet howled down the runway and lifted smoothly into the air. Bayport vanished under the clouds, and the pilot headed the aircraft southwest.

"We'll land at Houston International this afternoon," Pierce announced.

"And how far is the Big Thicket from there?" asked Joe.

"The airport's north of Houston," Pierce replied. "We'll be driving east some sixty miles, past Liberty County into Hardin."

"I can't wait," Joe declared. "Maybe you could tell us more about it, professor."

19

Pierce grinned, pleased with the boys' interest. "I could spend *months* talking about the Big Thicket. I think you'd better see the place first, though. After a couple of days exploring, you'll have questions to ask you can't imagine right now."

"The way things are going," Frank said wryly, "we may not have much time for sightseeing. Whoever wants you out of the way knows you're coming back from Bayport today. We can probably expect more trouble soon."

Pierce leaned back and rubbed a hand wearily over his face. "I don't know why this is happening," he declared. "Our work in the Thicket is vital. I wish Nelson Zeigler could understand that once the area is gone, it won't come back again!"

He stared out the window, and Frank exchanged a quick look with his brother. All they'd heard about the man seemed true. He was more concerned with preserving the Big Thicket than guarding his own life.

The boys left Pierce to his thoughts and joined Chet in exploring the cabin of the plane. There was room to move about and instead of cramped rows of seats, the jet had reclining easy chairs bolted to a carpeted floor. There was even a small, well-equipped kitchen, which Chet investigated at length while the Hardys looked at a library on the environment, and a computer terminal. At the rear of the cabin were small compartments complete with double-decker beds.

"A person could almost live in this thing," exclaimed Joe. "It wouldn't be too bad, either!"

"The professor says the NCG keeps their jet in use all the time," Frank commented. There's some vital ecological crisis popping up around the world almost every day."

"Anybody want something to drink to go with this chicken?" Chet called from the kitchen. "I see orange soda and lemonade in the refrigerator."

Joe looked at his watch and shook his head. "It's barely 10:30, Chet. Not even *close* to lunch."

"Hu-unh, you're wrong." Chet held up a drumstick and grinned. "I just checked with the pilot. That's Nashville off to our right. We're in another time zone and that means it's *eleven*-thirty."

You're half right, anyway," Frank said. "Only we're going west, not east. That means it's an hour *earlier*, not later. It's only 9:30 now."

"It is?" Chet shrugged and poked his hand in the basket for more chicken. "Oh, well, travel always makes me hungry."

"So does *not* traveling," said Joe. He sighed and started back for the kitchen. "Come on, Frank, we might as well join him. If we don't, there won't be anything left but bones. . . ."

Air traffic was heavy over Houston, and the jet circled lazily over the broad Gulf of Mexico to await airport clearance. The day was bright and clear and the water shimmered blue-green below them.

Finally, the plane touched down and rolled to a stop on the non-commercial side of the airfield. The twin jets whined into silence, and the pilot came back to open the hatch. Leaving the air-conditioned plane for the hot, sultry Texas air was almost like walking out of a freezer into a furnace.

"You'll get used to it," Professor Pierce grinned, noticing the boys' discomfort. "It's not even summer here yet."

He introduced them to a man named Harrison Baker, who was waiting for them. Baker, lean, blond, and in his early forties, was dressed in a lightweight khaki shirt and trousers.

"Here's the man who can answer your questions about the Big Thicket's part in the Civil War," Pierce explained. "Harrison's the best historian around, and knows everything there is to know about Texas."

"Well, almost everything." Baker grinned.

He directed the group to a sturdy-looking car that had seen plenty of use, and moments later they were driving through the heavy airport traffic.

Frank and Joe noticed that the historian seemed preoccupied with something. When he turned east toward Big Thicket Country, they found out why.

"I hate to greet you with bad news," Baker told Professor Pierce. "But after your phone call last night, considering what happened up in Bayport . . ."

"Go on," Pierce sighed. "I don't think you can surprise me anymore."

Baker cleared his throat. "Nelson Zeigler held a press conference this morning in Beaumont. He said you don't represent conservation interests at all—that you're really working for one of his rivals. He claims they're paying you off to keep him from oil and timber rights in the Thicket."

"What!" Pierce went rigid with anger. "He can't get away with a statement like that!"

Baker shook his head. "You know how people are. Many of them will believe it simply because it's printed in the paper."

"Well, plenty of them won't," Pierce growled. "I can tell you that. No one's ever questioned my honesty, and if Nelson Zeigler thinks he can —*Baker, look out!*"

Pierce's warning came as a big, eighteen-wheel truck burst out of a side road to their left and headed straight toward them. Baker jerked the wheel frantically to the right. The front of the truck slammed the rear of his car, sending it veering wildly across the road. Joe grabbed for support and went flying into Frank.

There was a harsh, high-pitched screech of metal against metal as the truck tried to force them off the road. Joe caught a flash of dull black paint and a dark, tinted window as Baker fought for control. The historian clutched the wheel and went through the gears, slamming the accelerator nearly through the floor.

The car lunged forward with a sudden burst of power. Baker shifted gears again, and left the eighteen-wheeler far behind.

"We're all right now," Frank said shakily. "They don't have the power to catch up."

"Stop as soon as you can and notify the police!" Pierce snapped.

Baker turned to him, his face drained of color. "It won't do any good," he said bitterly. "They'll probably get away, and I doubt if they even know who hired them for the job. If they're ever caught, they'll claim it was an accident."

He looked solemnly at the Hardys and Chet. "Welcome to the Big Thicket, boys."

3   *The Big Bite!*

Frank and Joe awoke early to find Chet already gone.

"That's not like him," said Frank. "I wonder what he's up to now?"

"One of two things," grinned Joe, running a comb through his hair. "Breakfast, or some new hobby he's discovered. He was pretty busy last night after supper. I think he went through everything in Professor Pierce's collection."

"I don't blame him," Frank declared. "Boy, this house is like a museum. You could spend a whole month here and never get tired of it."

Joe had to agree. The famed naturalist lived in a sprawling, old-fashioned house set in a grove of ancient oaks. Spanish moss covered the trees like shaggy beards. Inside, the rooms were filled with books, antiques and vibrant paintings of extinct wildlife.

Frank and Joe discovered Chet in the yard, in a thicket of pepper vines. He was on his hands and knees, searching the ground intently. By his side was a box filled with plastic dishes containing dirt.

"Hey, Chet," Frank called out, "what are you doing?"

Chet looked up, startled. "A little conservation work, that's all. Some experiments. Uh, you guys going to breakfast?"

"Professor Pierce said he'd be tied up all morning," Frank recalled. "There's supposed to be a cafe off the town square."

Chet frowned in thought. "You think we ought to leave the professor alone?"

"He'll be careful, I'm sure," Joe said. "Besides, we can't unravel this mystery if we stick around the house."

Frank and Chet nodded in agreement.

The town of Black Cypress Creek was in the heart of the Big Thicket. Main Street bordered an old town square with a weathered granite courthouse situated in the middle. The three friends passed a bank, several shops and a hardware store before they located the Armadillo Cafe. The pleasant smells of breakfast drifted out into the street. Joe opened the door, then stopped in his tracks and stared.

"Hey, guys!" he exclaimed, "I think we're in the wrong century!"

"If we are," Chet sighed, "I'm staying."

Half the cafe's tables were occupied by girls in their late teens, each one wearing an old-fashioned billowing gown of the 1860s. As the boys sat down, they all looked up and cheered.

"Wow," Frank said, "I never saw so many pretty girls in all my life!"

"Must have something to do with the celebration," Joe grinned. "I don't imagine they do this every day."

Frank passed menus around, and Chet set his carton of dishes against the wall. After the three had ordered, a slender girl in blue walked up to their table. She had sparkling green eyes and light blonde hair.

"Hi," she smiled. You must be Frank and Joe Hardy and Chet Morton. I'm Marilyn Baker. My dad drove you in last night."

"That's right," Frank said. "Please sit down and join us."

"I'll try," the girl frowned. "I don't know how those fine 19th century ladies put up with all these skirts. Okay—there, now." Marilyn sighed, then leaned intently across the table. "Some of my friends want to meet you," she said, "but I had to talk to you first. Dad told me what happened. He didn't want to, but I saw the side of the car. Mom's in Dallas with my aunt, and he doesn't like me to worry."

"Your dad did a great job of driving," Chet said. "If it hadn't been for him, we wouldn't have made it."

"Chet's right," Frank agreed.

Marilyn bit her lip. "Dad's pretty worried. He and Professor Pierce are good friends." She hesitated, and looked over her shoulder. "Listen—I know why you're here. I hope you can help stop this awful business before the professor gets hurt."

"Does anyone else know we're investigators?" Joe asked.

"Not yet." Marilyn shook her head. "But just you wait. Everyone in town will know before noon. People have a way of finding out things in this place. You wouldn't believe it."

"You can help us by not telling anyone," Joe said. "Also, by pointing us in the right direction."

"I'll do whatever I can. Oh, hey — " She looked up suddenly and grinned. "Joe and Frank, Chet, this is Bea Sterling and E.D. Girls, these are the guys visiting our fair city."

The group exchanged greetings as the boys' breakfast of waffles, ham, and orange juice arrived. Bea's hair was a darker blonde than Marilyn's. She had blue eyes and a winning smile. E.D. was tall and thin, with enormous brown eyes and black hair. From the look on Chet's face, it was clear he was instantly taken with the girl.

"E.D.?" he asked at once. "Does that stand for something?"

The other girls laughed. "It stands for Eleanora Doreen," she said ruefully. "Eleanora Doreen Threader. That's why I shortened it to E.D."

Chet stared at the girl. "I like Eleanora Doreen."

"You do?" E.D. looked astonished.

"Are you three going to be in town for the pageant?" asked Bea. "We could sure use your help. Every boy wants to be a Jayhawker. We don't have enough Rebels."

"You can count us in!" Chet said excitedly.

"We'd like to," Frank added.

"Hey, Mr. Morgan," Bea waved across the room. "I've got some new recruits!"

A man rose from behind the costumed girls and made his way across the room. He had thick, curly hair salted with gray, and even, well-tanned features. Joe guessed he was over forty, but he appeared to be in excellent physical condition.

Bea made the introductions. "If you ask them real nice," she said, "they just might join your Confederate army."

"Terrific!" Morgan boomed and shook hands with the boys. "In case Bea didn't tell you, I'm the so-called pageant director. Honest, guys, I'm only crazy part of the year." The girls laughed, and Morgan raised a hand for attention. "Hate to break this up, but we've got a rehearsal to run through. You boys are staying with Martin Pierce, right? Let's get together. We could really use your help." He turned and clapped his hands. "Okay, gang, finish up. I want fourteen Southern belles on the courthouse steps in five minutes!"

The girls groaned, but started pushing back chairs and gathering their skirts.

Frank looked curiously at Marilyn. "Now, how did *he* know where we were staying?"

"I told you," Marilyn said dryly, "there aren't any secrets in Black Cypress Creek."

"I could name a couple," Joe muttered.

"What does Mr. Morgan do," asked Frank, "when he isn't directing pageants?"

"He's a successful businessman, one of the

31

richest men in the county," E.D. replied. "But you'd never know it. And he's the best pageant director we ever had."

Marilyn rose and struggled with her outfit. "I hope I'll see you all later. Everyone usually goes down to Pop's Malt Shop after supper. You'll know me right off. I'll be the girl in an everyday shirt and jeans."

"We'll look forward to it," said Joe. "Maybe we can —" He stopped, catching the look on Bea's face. "Hey, what's wrong?"

"Oh, no," she said under her breath. "Bad news." She glanced toward the door. "It's Lew Hawks and Shiner Black."

"Who are they?" Chet asked.

"I think bullies is the right word," Marilyn said darkly. "Or maybe jerks. They don't have anything to do but look for trouble."

Frank and Joe watched the pair cross the room. They were lean young men in blue jeans, worn plaid shirts and timber boots. One had a thin, pinched face and a broken nose. The other, the larger of the two, wore a short-billed cap atop his shaggy, brown hair. He glanced at Chet, then grinned crookedly at E.D.

"What are you doing with Tubby here?" he leered. "I don't like my girlfriend hanging around with someone else."

"Girlfriend!" E.D. gasped. "I wouldn't even speak to you on the street, Lew Hawks!"

"Well, *I* say you are," Lew boasted.

"You'd better move on," said Chet, pulling himself up to his full height. "You heard what she said."

Lew laughed aloud. "Don't bother me, Fatso."

"Don't call me names!" Chet said angrily.

Frank sensed Chet was scared stiff, but knew his friend would never back away. He saw Lew doubling his fists at his sides.

"All right, hold it," Frank said, stepping up to the bully.

"You keep out of this!" Lew warned. He swung wildly at Frank, but the boy ducked under the blow. Chet lowered his shoulders and came at the bully, legs churning in a blur. His head hit the larger boy solidly in the stomach. Lew gasped, and flailed his arms in surprise. Then, tripping backward, he fell heavily on Chet's carton of dishes. He shook his head and pulled himself erect, clearly bent on revenge.

Suddenly, Lew's jaw fell. His eyes widened as he tore frantically at his trousers. He let out a yell and danced crazily about the room, then knocked over a chair and bolted out the front door. His friend stared in surprise, then beat a hasty retreat.

"Wow!" Joe exclaimed. "What got into him?"

Chet ran to his carton and threw up his hands. "He ruined everything," he cried furiously. "I'll have to start all over!"

"Start all over with what?" Frank asked. "What did you—" He looked past his friend and stared. "No wonder that guy got out of here fast. This place is crawling with ants! Chet—?"

"It's part of my study of the environment," Chet defended himself. "Preserving endangered species."

"Huh?" Frank looked puzzled. "But ants aren't endangered—there are billions of them!"

"Sure, there are *now*," Chet said. "But remember what the professor said about passenger pigeons? No one thought they'd be extinct, either. You just never can tell!" Chet tried to look serious, but Frank's incredulous face was too much. He burst out laughing.

4 A Strange Intruder

Frank, Joe, and Chet were still laughing when they left the restaurant. The girls had helped Chet retrieve his ants, and the owner of the cafe seemed more than a little relieved when the door shut behind the trio.

Finally Frank groaned. "Boy, I fell right into that one," he said to Chet. "Now, tell us, what were you really doing with all those ants?"

"Don't you remember?" Chet said. "I collect ants. I have various types of them back home. But I didn't have any of these, so I collected a few to take back."

Frank grinned. "I forgot. That was about three hobbies back, wasn't it? Before stamps, tropical fish, and baseball cards."

"I was just playing around with *that* stuff,"

Chet said firmly. "I'm *serious* about ants."

"It looked to me as if you were pretty serious about that tough guy at the cafe," Joe said, clapping his friend on the back. "I think he got the surprise of his life when you gave him the old goal-line block."

"I didn't like him talking to E.D. that way," Chet muttered. "She's a real nice girl."

"I have an idea she likes you, too," Joe declared.

"Aw, I don't know about that," Chet shrugged, turning red clear up to his ears.

Joe grinned at his friend's expression. His smile was cut short, however, as they approached the professor's house, and spotted two black cars parked in front.

"Uh-oh," Frank said, "looks like we've got company. I wonder what's up?"

Before they reached the front door, they could hear angry voices from inside. Stopping in the hall before the study, they saw an enormous man in a gray silk suit shaking his fist at Pierce.

"You have no right to accuse me of any such thing," the man fumed. "I won't stand for it, Pierce. You'd better get that through your head!"

"Accuse you!" Pierce snapped. "Every newspaper in the state says you think I'm a crook, working for your competitor instead of the Big

Thicket. That's a lie and you know it!"

"Is it?" the man growled. "How do I know it's not the truth?" The man was six-five or more and built like a bear. He towered over Pierce, while hands the size of hams doubled threateningly at his sides. "My sources tell me you've been paid off to keep my company out of the Thicket!"

"Mr. Zeigler, Professor—" For the first time, the boys saw that there was another man in the room. He had even features, a medium build, and thinning hair. "Gentlemen," he said calmly, "a lot of harsh words have been said on both sides. I think we all need to sit down and talk this over."

Zeigler glared. "What do you mean, both sides, Turner? Have you forgotten whom you work for?"

"No, I haven't," Turner said evenly. "I simply think we can accomplish more if we don't shout at one another."

"At least someone in your company's making sense," Pierce muttered.

"Now, look here," Zeigler bellowed, turning on the professor again. "I'll have you know I'm a reasonable man. No one has ever said I wasn't the—" He stopped suddenly, noticing the three boys in the hall. "Hah! I know who you are," he shouted. "Don't think I don't!" He pointed an accusing finger at Frank, Joe and Chet. "How do you expect me to talk things over with you, Pierce, when you're bringing in *snoops* to spy on me!"

"We're not snoops, Mr. Zeigler," Frank said evenly.

"And we're here because someone has been threatening Professor Pierce's life."

"Like just last night, for instance," Pierce said tightly. "That truck of yours tried to run us off the road. Ask these three—they were nearly killed, too."

Zeigler's face clouded in a fury. "I had nothing to do with that," he boomed, "or any other of those so-called attempts on your life!"

"So-called!" Pierce gasped in disbelief. "I've been shot at, run off the road—"

"I've had enough of this," Zeigler growled. "Come on, Turner, we're getting out of here."

"I'll—be along in a minute," Turner answered.

"Do whatever you like," Zeigler said, storming out of the room.

"Wow," Joe breathed, "that man's got a temper that won't quit!"

"He's not like that at all," said Nelson Zeigler's aide. "Really. But this business has him pretty upset." He stepped forward and offered his hand. "I'm Turner Fields. I work for Mr. Zeigler. At least, I *guess* I do. I may be out of a job right now, for all I know."

Frank, Joe and Chet shook his hand. Pierce eased himself down in a chair. "He'll leave you alone if he has any sense. You're the only man in Zeigco we can talk to any more."

Turner Fields frowned. "Mr. Zeigler is hotheaded sometimes, professor. But he's *not* behind these threats. You've got to believe that."

Frank looked at Fields. "No one has any proof that he's responsible, sir. But if Mr. Zeigler is not involved, who is? That's what we're here to find out."

"I have no idea," Fields said. "I only know Nelson Zeigler is not that kind of a man."

"That's what I thought, too," Pierce said glumly. "Now, I'm not at all sure." He stood up and turned. "If you folks will excuse me, I have work to do upstairs."

He left, and Fields shook his head sadly. "I have to say I don't blame him for the way he feels. Especially after that story Mr. Zeigler gave to the papers."

"Do you have any idea where he got it?" Joe asked.

"No," Fields shrugged. "I wish I did. But Mr.

Zeigler wouldn't tell me. I don't think he trusts me anymore. As I said, I have a feeling my days at Zeigco are numbered. I'm very pleased to have met you boys. Now, I'd better try to catch up with the boss."

He walked out of the study, through the hall, and out to his car.

"I don't think I'd like his job," Chet said. "Working for that Zeigler character for one day would be all I could handle."

"He seems pretty hard to get along with, all right," Frank mused. Then he looked thoughtfully at Joe and Chet. "We've got our work cut out for us. Nelson Zeigler's our number-one suspect, but we can't prove a thing. Anyone could be responsible for those attempts on the professor's life."

"And even if Zeigler's behind it," Joe added, "you can bet he wasn't even close to Professor Pierce when anything happened."

"That's right," Frank agreed. "He would have accomplices. And it's our job to find out who they are."

Frank, Chet and Joe spent the afternoon and early evening trying to pin down any clues that might lead them to the professor's mysterious assailant. Joe and Chet went over copies of the threatening letters and carefully inspected the area where the phone lines had been cut. Frank took the professor's Jeep and a hand-drawn map, and drove to the spot where someone had shot at Pierce in the woods. Then he checked the logging road where a car had tried to run down his host. As the boys suspected, too much time had passed for any evidence to remain. Besides, the local sheriff and his men had already searched the areas thoroughly.

"Well, we gave it a good try," Joe said later that night. "It looks like we have nothing to go on, though."

"We'll have to wait until someone tries again," Chet said.

Frank shook his head. "Don't even think about that," he said tightly. "We can't let that guy have another chance!"

It was nearly ten o'clock and the three friends were in their beds on the second floor. Frank had just turned off the lamp on his night table. A pale square of moonlight patched the floor.

"We'd better do something real soon," Joe said in the dark. "Did you see the professor at supper? He knows he ought to stay close to the house, but he doesn't like that at all. He keeps talking about work that needs to be done out in the Thicket."

"And the more he goes outside, the more exposed to danger he's going to be," Chet added.

"He sure won't stay cooped up forever," Frank agreed. "Which means one of us will have to stick close to him when he's out. We'll make up a schedule in the morning. I don't know what else we can—hey, what was that!" Frank sat up abruptly and stared into the dark. "Joe, Chet—did you see it!"

"I did," Joe responded. "Some kind of a—a light flashed on the wall in the hall. Right by the stairs!"

"It could have been a passing car," Chet suggested.

"Except there weren't any cars going by," Frank said. "Come on, but be careful."

He tiptoed out of the room and into the hall, Chet and Joe at his heels. At the head of the stairs he paused, waving the others to silence. He listened a long moment. At first there was nothing, only the wind brushing branches against the house. Then a sound was heard from below. It was a deep, faraway sound—as if a gigantic heart were pounding somewhere beneath the earth. Frank glanced at Joe and Chet. His throat was dry as dust. The sound was heard again. He took a deep breath and started slowly down the stairs.

His bare feet on the carpeted steps were too loud in his ears. The strange sound from below stopped. Had the intruder heard them? Was he waiting for them?

The moon lit the wooden floor below. Frank reached the bottom of the stairs. He could hear Joe breathing behind him. Carefully, he edged around the corner and peered along the darkened hall. *The light—there it was again! And it came from Professor Pierce's study!*

Frank's heart pounded against his chest. He gripped Joe's arm, signaling him to wait, then crept slowly forward on his hands and knees. Now he could hear the strange, pounding sound again. Light flashed from the open door of the study. Hair rose on the back of Frank's neck. Another foot . . . and then another. . . . Scarcely daring to breathe, he stood up and peered around the door into the room.

He cried out in alarm as another pair of eyes met his. He was jerked back from the door. Powerful hands reached out from the darkness to grip his throat. Frank gasped for air as the intruder began dragging him over the floor toward the window. . . .

5 Deadly Waters

Joe blinked in astonishment as Frank cried out and disappeared before his eyes. The sounds of a terrible struggle reached his ears. A chair splintered, and a lamp went crashing to the floor. Joe gritted his teeth and plunged into the darkened study. Two figures were locked together before the window. Joe had no time to think—one of the figures was his brother, the other an intruder.

He ran headlong at the two shadows, leaped off the floor and threw himself in the middle of the fight. His weight forced the pair to the ground. The prowler yelled in surprise and flailed out blindly in the dark. His fist caught Joe on the shoulder. Frank broke loose and tried to pin the stranger's arms. The man pushed him aside, kicked out at Joe and sprang free.

"He's getting away!" Joe shouted. Frank grabbed at a pair of legs. Again, the intruder broke away, lashed out desperately and bolted out the window.

"Joe, Chet—somebody get the switch!" Frank yelled.

An instant later, the study was flooded with light. The Hardys stared at each other, then scrambled to their feet. Chet stood beside the switch, a long piece of firewood hefted against his shoulder like a baseball bat.

"Wh—where is he?" Chet demanded. "Where did he go?"

Without a word, Joe grabbed the makeshift weapon from Chet and ran into the hall for the door.

"Careful!" Frank warned. "Watch yourself out there!"

Just then, the professor appeared in his robe. His eyes went wide as he took in the scene.

"What on earth happened in here!" he exclaimed. "I heard all the shouting and—and—"

"We had an unexpected visitor," Frank said tightly. He rubbed a hand gingerly over his throat. "Boy, whoever he was, he was strong. I thought I was in pretty good shape, but that guy had muscles on his muscles!" He glanced at the overturned chair, the broken lamp, and the books scattered about. "Professor, do you see anything missing?" he asked. "There was a weird, pounding noise—we all heard it upstairs."

"I think I know what he was doing," Pierce said, "but I can't imagine why." He went to his knees and studied the floor behind his desk. A corner of the rug was turned back to reveal a thick circle of metal.

"That's a drop safe, isn't it?" Chet asked.

"That's what it is," Pierce told him. He looked up and shrugged at the two boys. "Only I don't keep anything in it worth stealing. Some notes for a book on the Big Thicket, a few personal papers, and some historical maps of the area Harrison Baker and I put together." He spread his hands, bewilderment crossing his features. "Everything in there is perfectly worthless to anyone else. I keep things in the safe only to protect them from fire."

"Someone thinks what you have is worth stealing," Frank said grimly. "There—look at that!" He bent and retrieved a heavy mechanic's hammer.

Underneath the desk, he found a tempered steel chisel and several layers of thick toweling and foam rubber. "He tried to knock off the combination lock with a hammer and chisel," Frank explained. "And he used the toweling and rubber to muffle the noise. Not a very professional job—he came prepared to force the safe. Which means he doesn't know how to crack a combination."

"Sir, who knows you have a safe in your study?" Chet asked.

"Probably many people," Pierce said dryly. "I bought it through a catalog in the hardware store. There wasn't any reason to keep it a secret."

"Could we take a look at the contents in the morning?" Frank asked. "There might be a clue as to why someone thinks your notes and maps are important."

"Fine," Pierce replied, "but I certainly can't imagine what would be there of use to you. Conservationists want everyone to know what they're doing. We don't try to keep our work a secret."

Frank, Chet and the professor glanced up as Joe walked back into the room. "It's pitch-dark out there," he said flatly. "The only thing I found was his flashlight where he dropped it. There are tracks under the window, leading away from the house. We might be able to follow them in the morning."

"Right," Frank said. "Professor, I'd suggest you call the sheriff and let him know what's happened, though I don't think he'll find a trace of our prowler. Joe, Chet—let's double check all the doors and windows and get some sleep."

"Sleep!" Joe exclaimed. "Who's going to sleep with a prowler lurking around out there!"

After breakfast, Frank, Joe and Chet left the house to follow the intruder's tracks. The ground beneath the big oaks was fairly damp, and it was easy to trace the heavy prints.

"He stood right here," Joe pointed angrily, "right beside the house. Just waiting for us to go to bed and turn off the light!"

"Whoever he is, he's got nerve," Frank remarked. "He didn't even wait until we went to sleep." He glanced curiously at his brother. "It's real peculiar, you know? This time he wasn't after the professor at all. He was after something Pierce had."

"I guess we'll know the answer when we get to the bottom of this," Joe said.

"Hey, come here," Chet called out. "I found the spot where the burglar crossed the yard and climbed the fence!"

Frank and Joe joined Chet behind the professor's home. Only a few feet past the cedar fence, the woods were thick with natural cover. Spanish moss dripped nearly to the earth, and the ground was carpeted with bright green ferns.

"Wow," Chet explained, "I feel like I'm in a Daniel Boone movie!"

"I wish old Daniel was here," Frank muttered. "Maybe *he* could follow this trail."

"Right here," Joe shouted. "Take a look!"

Frank and Chet pushed a tangle of vines aside to join him. Joe pointed at the ground. "The intruder came this way. The tracks lead over there. He was moving pretty fast, too—and in the dark, remember."

The boys followed the footprints a good thirty yards through the trees. Suddenly, the giant oaks gave way to a narrow river. The water was deep and still, dark as a black mirror. Heavy branches overhead choked out the sun. Only a ghostly yellow light reached the surface.

"Wow," Chet said in an awed whisper, "we've hardly left the house, and we're in the middle of a deserted wilderness!"

"Hi, what are you guys doing?" a voice suddenly called out behind him. "We've been looking all over for you."

Chet turned, startled, to see the three girls coming toward him up the path by the river.

Marilyn, Bea and E.D. were dressed in blue jeans, boots, and bright yellow T-shirts that read: JAYHAWKERS AND REBELS CELEBRATION.

"You just taking a morning hike or what?" Bea asked.

"Not exactly," Frank told her. "We had a little trouble last night." He quickly explained what had happened and how they were trying to track the prowler. The girls looked wide-eyed, then bent to study the tracks.

"I can tell you one thing," E.D. announced. "He was wearing swamp boots. See? Like the ones I have on." She pulled up the cuff of her jeans. "That's not much help, I guess. Everybody around here wears them."

"They're waterproof, and high-topped to guard against snakes," Bea added.

"Snakes?" Chet asked. "What kind of snakes?"

"Oh, just about every poisonous snake you can find in the United States," Marilyn said absently. "Corals, copperheads, cottonmouth water moccasins, canebrake rattlers . . ."

"Great," Joe groaned.

"If we're going to follow these tracks any farther," Frank said, "we'll have to get across the river. Is there a bridge nearby?"

"No," Marilyn shook her blonde hair. "But I

know how we can get across. Come on, I'll show you."

Fifty yards upstream, she stopped and pointed through a stand of green willows. Two flat-bottomed boats with square prows were pulled up ashore.

"They're *pirogues*," Marilyn explained. "They're the only kind of boats you can use in shallow marshes. These two belong to Mr. Waldorp, who likes to fish. I know he won't mind if we borrow them."

"Fine," Frank said, "let's go."

He slid one *pirogue* into the water for himself, Chet, and E.D., and Joe, Bea and Marilyn took the other. In moments, they were gliding noiselessly across the dark river.

"We'd better go south," Frank called out. "We walked pretty far upstream."

"Right," Joe answered. The two boats slid down the shadowy channel. A thick stand of swamp grass choked half the river to the left. As the boats passed by, two snowy egrets exploded into the air with loud cries. Joe nearly jumped out of his skin at the sudden motion.

"Happens all the time," Bea laughed. "You'll get used to it."

"I hope so," Joe said. "I guess you've lived here all your life, right?"

"Just about. We've been exploring every spot within miles since we were kids."

"And you can still get lost five minutes from town," Marilyn added. "Believe me. I've done it."

"I'll bet," Joe said. "I don't know how you even—"

"Watch out," Bea shrieked suddenly. *"Get us out of here—fast!"*

Joe jerked around and looked to his left. He tried to speak but the words stuck in his throat. An enormous shape was gliding toward them from the bank. At first it looked like a giant, shaggy-barked log. Then, the "log" opened its yawning jaws and showed glistening rows of teeth!

Joe frantically churned the water with his oars. He didn't dare look at the monster—he was sure one glance would be enough to finish him off.

"Hurry," Marilyn cried out, "it's coming right at us!"

Joe's heart sank. The shore looked a hundred miles away. He knew they'd never make it. Desperately, he searched the way ahead—the water, the trees and the low-hanging branches.

"The vines, up there!" he shouted. "When we get right under them, jump for it!"

"They're too high," Bea protested. "I can't reach that far!"

"Just try," Joe shouted. "There's no other way!" His arms ached as he swept the small boat ahead. Frank yelled from the other *pirogue*, but his words were lost. Suddenly, Marilyn screamed a warning. Joe saw the shadow of the alligator's jaw across the boat and knew the huge creature was nearly upon them.

"Jump!" he shouted hoarsely. "Jump *now!*"

Wood splintered behind him as the monster's jaws snapped shut. Joe leaped at the last instant, stretching for the vines overhead. He grasped the woody growth, his legs dangling inches above the water. Then he pulled himself up. Glancing back, he saw the giant amphibian sink below black water and disappear. The wrecked boat was gone. Looking up, he saw Bea clinging wide-eyed to a branch high above, and wondered how she'd gotten that far. Marilyn clung precariously to the vine next to his.

"You Tarzan, me Jane," she grinned weakly. All color was drained from her face.

"Huh-uh." Joe shook his head. "You Jane, me scared clear out of my wits!"

6   The Serpent's Message

After Joe, Bea and Marilyn were safely aboard the remaining boat, Frank paddled quickly to shore. No one was sure the giant creature wouldn't return and try again.

"Did you see the *size* of that thing?" Joe exclaimed. "I thought a nuclear sub was trying to surface!"

"It was big," Frank said, "but it wasn't *that* big."

"Oh, no?" Joe gave his brother a withering look. "It wasn't trying to eat *your* boat!" He turned to Marilyn and Bea. "Are you two all right? You're not hurt or anything?"

"I'll let you know tomorrow," Bea said shakily. "If my hair doesn't turn completely white overnight I'll be fine."

Marilyn shook her head. "I've read all the stories in the papers. I'm not sure I believed them until now. You won't see *me* in a boat again—not until someone gets rid of that monster."

"Gets rid of it how?" asked Chet. "With a cannon?"

"What puzzles me," Frank said, "is how anything could grow to that size without being noticed. No one ever saw this creature until a couple of months ago."

"Anyone who's lived out here for a while can answer that," E.D. spoke up. "The Thicket's full of secrets. Even the old-timers say there are places no one's ever seen. There's no telling what's out there."

"So a monster like that could live in hiding for years," Chet finished, "until it decided to come out and get acquainted."

"Right," agreed E.D. "Thousands of creeks run through the swamp and disappear. It's almost impossible to—oh, look, someone's coming!"

Everyone turned to see a dusty blue car stop under the trees. A gold star was visible on its side. A lean-bodied man in khakis stepped out and walked toward them.

"It's Sheriff Vard Proctor," said Bea. "Come on, we'd better tell him about that 'gator."

The girls introduced the Hardy boys and Chet. Joe reported what had happened, and the others told everything they could recall about the monster.

Sheriff Proctor took notes on a small pad, then removed his dark glasses and rubbed his eyes. "Guess we'll have to call this one a true sightin'," he drawled, "being as how there were six of you who saw it." He shook his head and grinned. "You have no idea how many monster calls we get."

"This was the real thing, all right," Joe said grimly.

"Oh, I don't doubt it," said the sheriff. He squinted at the Hardy boys and Chet. "You three are the, uh—investigators staying with Pierce, aren't you? I got the professor's call last night. Right after sunup I followed those tracks from the house to the river. I guess you boys did the same."

"Yes, sir, we did," Frank told him. "We were going over to check the other side. As you know, we never made it across."

"Don't bother," the sheriff said evenly.

"There's nothing there to see."

"Nothing?" Joe looked puzzled. "The tracks just end?"

"You haven't been detecting down in this county as long as I have," Sheriff Proctor said wryly. "In a good part of the Big Thicket, walking is the worst way to get to where you're going. My guess is this prowler left by the river. Flat-bottom fishing boat, likely, with a light outboard motor. Plenty of 'em around."

"Which means we don't have a chance of finding him," Chet added.

"Now you've got it right," Sheriff Proctor said. He nodded at the girls and grinned at Frank, Joe and Chet. "See you folks around." He climbed into his car and vanished through the trees.

"You know what?" Joe said darkly. "I don't think he's real impressed with us, Frank."

Frank laughed. "I don't blame him. All we've managed to do is wrestle a prowler and run from an alligator."

"Huh!" Chet muttered. "You forgot being chased down the road by a truck. How much excitement do you guys want?"

Bea and E.D. had to go to the pageant office to paint posters and said goodbye at the professor's house, but Marilyn stayed with the boys.

Frank told Pierce how the prowler's tracks had vanished at the river. When he learned of their close call, the professor stared at the four young people in open wonder.

"Good heavens!" he exclaimed, "when I told you boys that story in Bayport, I had no idea you'd ever really *see* the creature!"

Once he was sure they were unhurt, his scientist's curiosity began to show: How long was the alligator? Could they guess the length of its teeth?

"When he was trying to eat the boat, I'd have said they were two feet long," Joe replied dryly. "But I suppose they were shorter than that."

Pierce chuckled, then turned serious again. "I've given a lot of thought to last night," he told the boys. "You asked me what the prowler might have wanted in my safe. I still can't come up with an answer." He paused and looked thoughtfully at Marilyn. "Maybe your father can think of something. We worked together on the historical data and maps."

"We can go over now and ask him, if you'd like," Marilyn suggested.

"Might be a good idea if you called from here," Pierce said. "If Vard Proctor's spread the word about that alligator attack all over the county . . ."

"Wow, you're right, professor," Marilyn groaned. "I'd better tell him I'm okay. He'll want to hear it from me!"

Harrison Baker lived next to the Armadillo Cafe, in one of the few homes near the square that hadn't been converted to a place of business. The big, two-story frame house was shaded by large magnolias and nearly covered by Virginia creeper vines. Baker met his daughter and her new friends on the steps, assured himself she was safe, and invited everyone inside.

"I'm glad you called," he said evenly. "You know how Proctor's stories start to grow."

They were sitting on the screened-in porch off the kitchen. Marilyn set a pitcher of lemonade and a plate of cookies on the table, much to Chet's delight.

"Martin called me after you left," Baker went on somberly. "We talked about the intruder and I have to agree with him. I can't imagine what a thief could possibly want with that material!"

Frank shrugged. "It was the only lead we had, and we wanted to follow it through."

Joe sipped his lemonade. "Sir, is there anything at all about the Thicket's history that's a—a secret of some kind? Something most people wouldn't know?"

Baker shook his head. "Absolutely not. Everything we know has been published somewhere or other. I'm responsible for a lot of it myself." He leaned back and squinted his eyes. "How much do you boys know about the history of the Big Thicket?"

Frank and Joe shrugged. "Not a lot," Frank replied. "The one book I've read didn't give a lot of history of the area."

"Well, I won't go back too far," Baker said. "I will tell you why we have the Jayhawkers and Rebels' celebration, and you can ask questions if you like. You all know about the Alamo, of course. Well, after the Mexican General Santa Anna won that battle in February of 1836, he turned his forces against Sam Houston. Houston beat Santa Anna at San Jacinto, six weeks later. But if he hadn't won, he was planning on hiding his troops in the Big Thicket." He paused to sip some lemonade, then continued. "Later, when Houston was an old man, he toured Texas, pleading with folks not to withdraw from the Union. Houston's sympathizers came to be known as Jayhawkers, and a good many holed up here during the Civil War. It was 'a rich man's war,' they said—they were poor people and had nothing to gain, no matter who won in the end. The Confederate troops tried time and time again to drive the Jayhawkers out of the swamps. Most of the time they failed. That's what our celebration is all about—the conflict between the Confederate army and the people of the Thicket."

"Wow, I didn't know any of that," Chet said.

"Tell them about the 'Lost Column,' Dad," Marilyn urged.

"Oh, right," said Baker. "That's the conflict we reenact every year. The Jayhawkers attacked a Confederate supply column in the Thicket. There was a fierce fight, and the Rebels were soundly beaten. A number of them escaped, but the whole column of wagons was lost. They simply sank in the swamp and disappeared."

"Where in the Thicket did this happen?" asked Joe.

A weary smile crossed Baker's face. "I wish I could say for sure. We know about where it is. But a miss is as good as ten miles in the swamp."

"That's a good story," Frank said. "I'd heard about the Jayhawkers, but I didn't really know who they were."

"The Lost Column is quite a tale," Baker agreed, "but I'm afraid that mystery doesn't help you much with yours."

"No," Joe began, "but it's a—" His words were lost as the sound of breaking glass came from the front of the house. Frank got to his feet first and ran into the hall. When the others arrived, he was staring at the shattered front door and a white plastic container on the floor.

"Who would dare do a thing like this?" Baker said angrily.

Frank picked up the plastic container. The lid was bound firmly with black tape.

"Careful," Joe warned.

Frank peeled the tape off, held the carton away from his body, and shook the contents to the floor.

Marilyn cried out in alarm. A slim-bodied snake, no more than eight inches long, slithered quickly across the floor. Black, yellow and red rings circled its body.

"Back, everybody," Baker snapped. "That's a coral snake and it's deadly!"

Chet grabbed a wastebasket and quickly trapped the snake underneath.

Frank unfolded a piece of paper that had fallen out of the container.

"'Harrison Baker,'" he read, "'stay away from Martin Pierce and his friends or you'll get what's coming to them!'"

"'His friends,'" Chet muttered. "I guess that means us."

"I don't believe this," said Joe. He shook his head in bewilderment. "It's as if someone is watching our every move."

7   *Feathers Fly*

Only moments after the glass in the front door had shattered, people began to gather on the Bakers' broad porch. Customers from the cafe came to stare. Shoppers ran across the square to join the crowd. Sheriff Proctor arrived and immediately questioned everyone in sight. As soon as they'd told their story, Frank, Joe and Chet left through the back door. Frank had called the professor to tell him what had happened and warned him to stay inside.

"It's kind of odd," Joe said curiously. "All those people came around and yet no one saw a thing!"

"I don't know," Frank shrugged. "Those trees

in the yard give plenty of cover. It wouldn't be hard to toss something through the door and disappear."

"No, I guess it wouldn't," Joe grumbled. "I don't like it, Frank. I still say someone knows everything we're doing."

Frank shook his head. "They don't know what we're doing, Joe. They know where we are and they've decided to try and scare us off—and frighten Mr. Baker at the same time."

"Well, it's not going to work!" Chet exclaimed. "Did you see Mr. Baker's face? Boy, is he mad! Whoever's behind all this had better—"

"*Chet, look out!*" Joe shouted.

Chet leaped out of the street as a faded yellow Jeep suddenly screeched around the corner, headed toward him, and then veered away at the last instant. The car made a quick turn and raced past them again. The driver and his passenger laughed and jeered, then went around a corner and disappeared.

"Did you see that?" Chet said angrily. "It was those two guys from the cafe, Lew Hawks and Shiner Black!"

"I don't think they like you, Chet," Frank said dryly.

"Oh, no?" Chet shook his fist at the empty

street. "Well, they'd better watch what they're doing!"

When the three friends arrived at Pierce's house, they found the professor carrying equipment into the hall. Besides canteens and packs, there were binoculars, tripods, and several cameras.

"Professor," Frank said curiously, "I don't have to be a detective to know you're planning a trip. Do you mind if I ask what's up?"

Pierce beamed. "You're right, that's exactly what I'm doing." He checked off an item on his list. "Have you ever heard of the ivory-billed woodpecker?"

"I think so," Joe said. "It's extinct, isn't it?"

"It's *supposed* to be extinct," Pierce corrected. Excitement gleamed in his eyes. "We're not all that certain that it is. Every year we get reports that these birds are still alive in the Big Thicket."

"And now someone's spotted one, right?" Frank said.

Pierce nodded. "A good friend called not half an hour ago. A fisherman got a picture of a bird with one of those instant cameras. My friend says it's the real thing!"

Frank exchanged a look with Chet and Joe. "Uh, it's none of our business, sir, and I know this is important to you. . ."

"I know, I know." Pierce interrupted. "You think it's dangerous for me to go wandering off like this. Well, I'm not going to stay cooped up in this house the rest of my life. Nelson Zeigler can threaten me all he wants!"

Frank saw there was no use trying to stop him. "If you're going after this woodpecker," he said, "we'd like to tag along, too, if you don't mind."

Professor Pierce grinned. "Why, I'd be delighted to have you. I knew exactly what you'd say about this trip. That's why I've already packed extra gear for the three of you!"

Before dawn, they were on the road in Pierce's Jeep, with a flat-bottomed aluminum boat hitched to a trailer behind. An hour later, they parked the Jeep and launched the boat in a dark lagoon.

"We're headed for a spot called Snapping Turtle Lake," Pierce explained. "It's just four or five miles on the map, but don't let that deceive you. It'll take a while to get there."

Joe sat in the stern of the small craft while Frank and Chet took seats in the bow. Professor Pierce sat in the middle, readying his camera.

He'd given Frank and Chet powerful binoculars and told them to keep their eyes open. Chet held a book open to a picture of the bird they were after.

"Boy, that doesn't look like any woodpecker I've ever seen," Chet declared.

"There's nothing else like it," Pierce told him.

The bird in Chet's book looked as big as a hawk. Its high, peaked crest was bright red, its feathers black and white.

"It says here that it always pokes holes in a pattern of a square." Chet said curiously. "Is that really true?"

"It's true," Pierce said. "Nobody's quite sure why."

The boat slid over black water under a heavy canopy of green foliage. A gray squirrel chattered in a loblolly pine, sending a lark sparrow into flight.

"Better spray yourself with some of this," Pierce warned, passing a bottle of insect repellent around. "There are plenty of mosquitoes here." A few moments later, the three companions saw he was right. The boat went underneath green palmetto fronds into a tangle of cypress trees and vines. The water was inky black and the sun peeked through the choking foliage in buttery shafts. All at once, mosquitoes attacked in droves. The bug spray helped, but the insects continued to whine about in dense clouds.

"Wow," Joe said, "you weren't kidding!"

"Wait until we hit the gnats *and* mosquitoes," Pierce said wryly.

A few moments later, the professor signaled Joe to stop the motor. The boat drifted ashore in the utter silence of the swamp.

"We'll have to take the channel to the right," Pierce said. "I just wanted you to see this spot while you're here." He stepped out of the boat and motioned to the boys to follow. "Walk where I walk," he warned them. "It may *appear* dry, but you could sink up to your waist in seconds. There," he pointed, pulling a tangle of vines aside, "take a look!"

At first, the young detectives saw nothing but a dark and gloomy hollow. Then, suddenly, Frank gave a low whistle. "Hey, that's really something!"

The boys stared in wonder at the sight. The dark bog was thick with multi-colored orchids clinging to the trees and vines.

"A place like this is called a baygall," Pierce explained, "because of the gallberry bushes and bay trees that grow here. Those orchids are, uh—let's see . . . wood orchids, snowy orchids and snake-mouth."

"I feel that I've traveled back in time about a million years," Chet whispered.

"I get the same sensation every time I come here," Pierce said. "You can almost—" He suddenly stood up straight. "Hold it, boys. Listen!"

Something big and heavy moved through the brush not ten yards away. Joe heard a low, throaty growl that raised the hairs on the back of his neck. Then a sharp, rapid noise sounded nearby.

Rrrrrh! Rrrrrh! Click-click-click-click!

There was a loud crash and clatter as something enormous swept brush and leaves aside and raced away.

"Wh—what on earth was that!" Chet exclaimed.

"A razorback hog," said Pierce. "A big one, three, maybe four, hundred pounds."

"What was that sound it made?" Joe asked.

"Just snapping its teeth," Pierce grinned. "Its tusks curve up from the bottom jaw and click on the teeth above. He couldn't get to us—they're too smart to get stuck in a baygall."

"*Now* you tell us," breathed Joe.

It was only nine in the morning when the boat reached Snapping Turtle Lake. Pierce called for quiet before they came out of the creek into the open. The motor went silent and the boys started rowing. Fog clung to the flat water ahead. The marshy lake was a ghostly forest of dead pines bearded with moss. Frank thought the trees looked like the masts of sunken ships. The sun overhead was white-hot.

"Row quietly and keep your eyes open," Pierce whispered. "Right around here is where that fellow spotted the ivory-bill."

Yellow irises dotted the far shores. A group of pure white herons took to the sky. At Pierce's direction, the boys guided the boat through shaggy trees. The professor perched in the bow, all of his cameras ready.

Chet's eyes ached from staring into the sun. He blinked and turned away, and almost missed the patch of red to his left.

"Professor, look," he pointed excitedly, "over there!"

Pierce grabbed the binoculars and focused on the trees. "That's it," he blurted, a grin spreading across his features. "Chet, you've found it! It's an ivory-billed woodpecker for sure! Paddle slowly, boys. Just let the boat drift as much as you can. I'll start getting some pictures."

Now they could see the bird clearly, perched atop a bare branch some thirty yards ahead. The professor's movie camera whirred as the boat drifted closer through veils of moss. Then Pierce set his movie camera aside and picked up a camera with a telephoto lens.

"I can't believe it," he whispered. "It's really there! I had a hunch they weren't all—"

The loud, throaty roar of a shotgun suddenly echoed across the lake. A second shot quickly followed the first. Pierce dropped his camera and stared in horror as the ivory-billed woodpecker exploded in a shower of feathers.

"No," he cried out. "Stop, stop—you can't!"

Suddenly, another boat burst through the nearby trees, its outboard roaring at full power. Two men were huddled near the stern. Frank grabbed his binoculars and followed the craft's twisting course. It circled the lake in a wide arc, then vanished around the bend, raising a froth of white spray.

Frank lowered his binoculars and faced the others. "They turned their heads away," he said grimly. "I couldn't tell who they were, but I saw something really interesting, professor."

"What? What?" Pierce demanded.

"A patch," Frank said. "One of them had a Zeigco Corporation patch on his shirt!"

8 Dark Threats

On the drive back from Snapping Turtle Lake, Professor Pierce was too angry to talk. He gripped the wheel of the Jeep and stared straight ahead. When they reached town, he passed his house and kept going.

"Professor," Joe said, "weren't you supposed to—"

"I know what I'm doing," Pierce said darkly. "I'm going to get this thing settled with Nelson Zeigler once and for all!"

"Sir, do you think that's a good idea?" Frank asked. "I mean, you're pretty upset over what happened."

Pierce didn't answer. He passed the courthouse and screeched to a stop in front of the

72

Lansdale Hotel. An instant later he was stamping up the steps and charging through the lobby, the young detectives right behind him.

"Uh-oh," Joe said to Frank. "Looks like we've got trouble. There's Mr. Zeigler."

Pierce had already spotted the man coming out of the dining room. Zeigler turned, startled, as the professor stormed up to him, both fists swinging. Zeigler was a much bigger man, and easily pushed the professor away. Frank and Joe stepped in to keep the two apart.

"What is this?" Zeigler blurted. "Have you gone crazy, Pierce!"

"Me?" Pierce raged. "I'd say it's the other way around. No one in his right mind would do a thing like this!" He reached in the pocket of his jacket and thrust a shaky hand at Zeigler.

Zeigler looked puzzled. "Wh—what's that? All I see is a handful of feathers."

"That's all there is," Pierce replied. "It used to be one of the rarest birds in the world—one we didn't even know still existed!"

"I don't understand." Zeigler shook his head. "What does this have to do with me?"

"Mr. Zeigler," Frank interrupted, "two men in a boat killed an ivory-billed woodpecker while we were watching. One of them had a Zeigco Corporation patch on his sleeve."

73

Zeigler's eyes narrowed. "So that's it. You think I had something to do with this."

"I don't *think* you did," Pierce shouted. "I *know* you did!"

"Well, you're wrong," Zeigler said flatly. "And you have no right at all to accuse me of such a thing."

"They were your people," Pierce snapped.

"If they were—which I strongly doubt—then you should report this to the sheriff." Zeigler's face clouded. "Anyway, you have no proof at all these men were my employees. It's not that hard to get a shirt with a Zeigco patch."

"Pardon me," a voice said over Joe's shoulder. "I don't like to butt in, professor, but I guess maybe I'd better."

Joe turned to see Rake Morgan, the pageant director they'd met at the cafe the day before.

Zeigler thrust out his chin. "What do you want? This is no business of yours."

"Yes, I think it is," Morgan said firmly. "I wasn't eavesdropping, but I couldn't help overhearing what you said. Many of us who live around here are concerned with what happens in the Big Thicket. We know what Professor Pierce is trying to do, and we don't like the kind of trouble that's been coming his way."

Zeigler bristled. "I've heard about all of this nonsense I want to hear!" He started off, but

Morgan blocked his way. He wasn't as big a man as Zeigler, but he'd kept himself in excellent physical shape.

"Move aside," Zeigler said darkly. "I'm warning you, fella."

Morgan looked at Pierce. "I was out doing business early this morning. I saw Mr. Zeigler behind the hotel. He was talking to two of his men. They were both wearing shirts with Zeigco patches."

Zeigler exploded with laughter. "Is that your evidence against me? Of course I was talking to my men. I've talked to a dozen of them today. I have geologists, surveyors, timber men — all kinds of people bringing me reports on the Big Thicket. So what!"

"The two men you talked to early this morning," Frank asked. "Can you tell us who they were, Mr. Zeigler?"

"No, I can't," Zeigler snapped. "I don't remember. And even if I did, it's none of your business, you young snoop!"

"Hah! That's what I thought," Pierce exclaimed. "Well, you can just tell your employees they're wasting their time out there, Zeigler. I'm going to do everything in my power to see that your company never gets oil and timber rights in the Thicket. As far as I'm concerned, the negotiations are finished!"

Zeigler's eyes opened wide. "You can't do that!"

"You just watch me," Pierce told him.

Zeigler glared at the professor, then turned and shook his fist at Rake Morgan. "This is all your fault, Mr. Troublemaker. I'll get even with you if it's the last thing I ever do!" He pushed Morgan roughly aside and stalked angrily out of the hotel.

Morgan shook his head. "I'm sorry, professor. Maybe I shouldn't have interfered. I just—"

"You didn't do a thing wrong," Pierce assured him. "It's about time I had it out with Zeigler. He's pushed me entirely too far."

Morgan looked at his watch. "It's close to seven-thirty. Why don't you all join me at the Armadillo Cafe? I'll treat everyone to steaks."

"You boys go on with Mr. Morgan," Pierce said wearily. "I'm not very hungry. And don't worry about me, okay? Zeigler won't try anything else today."

"Are you going back to the house?" Frank asked.

"Yes," Pierce assured him. He turned and walked across the lobby.

"He'll probably be okay," Frank said, "but you guys go on ahead. Bring me a cheeseburger from the cafe. I think I'll hang around for a while

76

outside the professor's house. Just in case."

"Good idea," Joe said.

Frank left, and Joe and Chet followed Rake Morgan across the lobby. He stopped to make a quick call, then led the boys outside and across the square. It was a hot, late spring evening, and the daylight was just beginning to fade.

"Boy, I don't think I ever saw anyone as mad as Mr. Zeigler," Chet sighed. "He's sure got it in for you, Mr. Morgan."

"I'm not worried," Morgan told him. "I can take care of myself. It's Professor Pierce who concerns me."

"I think Frank was right," Chet said. "One of us ought to be there. The way things are going . . ."

Joe nodded agreement.

"Oh, by the way," Morgan said suddenly, "in all the excitement I almost forgot. The reenactment of the Lost Column battle is tomorrow. E.D., Marilyn and Bea volunteered all three of you as soldiers." He saw their expressions and laughed. "So—unless you want to make three pretty girls angry, consider yourselves enlisted in the Army of the Confederacy."

"Wow, that's terrific!" Chet said.

"If everything goes all right with the professor, you can count us in," Joe said.

"Fine, fine! Now let's get ourselves some of those steaks!"

"That's the best idea I've heard all day," Chet exclaimed.

Joe and Chet were surprised to find Harrison Baker and Zeigler's aide, Turner Fields, seated at a corner table. Baker saw them and waved them over. "Come and join us," he said. "We were just getting ready to order."

Joe, Chet and Rake Morgan pulled up chairs. Morgan squinted at Fields. "You should have been over at the Lansdale Hotel," he said. "We just had a run-in with your employer."

"What are you talking about?" Fields asked curiously.

Morgan told Baker and Fields what had happened. Joe recounted the incident at the lake. Fields blinked in surprise, and Harrison Baker gripped his chair in anger.

"They—they killed an ivory-billed woodpecker? I can't believe it!"

"Well, it happened," Joe assured him. "And your boss is pretty mad, Mr. Fields. He even threatened to get even with Mr. Morgan."

Fields took a long swallow of iced tea and sank back wearily in his chair. "I just told Harrison here, and I might as well tell the rest of you. I don't work for Nelson Zeigler any more. I've been unemployed for about"—he glanced at his watch—"eight hours, I guess."

Chet blinked. "He fired you?"

"He sure did. He thinks I've taken Professor Pierce's side on this thing."

"From what I've heard, that's not true at all," Morgan said. "You're the only man at Zeigco who has tried to look at everything fairly."

"I'm afraid that's not enough for Mr. Zeigler," Fields sighed. "He demands a lot from his employees."

"Do you still think he's innocent?" Joe asked. "I know you did when we talked before."

"I—" Fields hesitated. "Yes, yes, I do," he said firmly. "Nelson Zeigler can be a very unreasonable man—but I don't think he'd do the things Pierce has accused him of doing."

"Someone's doing them," Joe pointed out.

"I know, I know." Fields ran a hand through his hair. "I just—can't believe Mr. Zeigler is involved. I wish I could have made him understand why I've taken such an interest in the conservation issues here. Oil and timber rights have been mishandled in this area in the past. It doesn't have to be that way. We can work in the Big Thicket without greatly disturbing its animal and plant life."

79

"Turner's shown a great interest in the Thicket," Baker told the others. "Particularly our rich history." He grinned at the bulging briefcase by Fields' chair. "That's the latest stack of books he's borrowed from me. By the time he leaves here, he's going to know more about the Thicket than I do."

"Not quite, I'm afraid," Fields said.

"I wish Nelson Zeigler was as interested in what's in the Thicket, as he is in what he can take out," growled Morgan.

"Has there ever been any—trouble, in areas where Mr. Zeigler has worked before?" Joe asked.

"Trouble? You mean like—" Fields shook his head firmly. "No, nothing like this has ever happened before, I assure you."

"And you've worked for him how long?"

"A little over nine years," Fields said bitterly. "And there's never been any—" Fields stopped as the door to the cafe jerked open. Sheriff Vard Proctor searched the room, then ran quickly up to their table.

"You'd better get over to your place fast," he told Morgan. "Someone just broke into your office and tore up everything in sight!"

9 "This Battle's Real!"

Rake Morgan doubled his fists in anger and bolted out of the cafe. Joe, Chet, Turner Fields and Harrison Baker followed the sheriff across the square. Street lamps burned along Main Street, but all the shops were dark.

"Mr. Morgan's office is over there," Proctor pointed. "Behind the courthouse to the left."

The boys saw it at once. The glass-front office was ablaze with lights. Gold letters on the window read: R. MORGAN INVESTMENTS. Joe and Chet stepped inside.

"Don't touch anything," Proctor warned. "Whoever did this may have left a clue."

"What do you mean *who*ever?" Morgan snapped. "It was those hoodlums who work for Zeigler!"

Morgan stamped about the office in a fury. File cabinets were open and papers were scattered over the floor. Chairs were overturned and pictures had been ripped off the walls.

"I want that man arrested," Morgan cried out. "Do your duty, sheriff!"

Vard Proctor cleared his throat. "Uh, we don't know that Mr. Zeigler had anything to do with this, Mr. Morgan. I can ask him some questions, of course—when he gets back in town."

Joe raised an eyebrow. "Mr. Zeigler's gone?"

"He drove off in that big black car of his half an hour ago," said Proctor.

"That's convenient," Morgan muttered.

"I'd appreciate it if you can tell me what's missing," Proctor said. "That might be a help."

Morgan grimaced. "I assure you there won't be anything missing at all. Zeigler did this only to get back at me!"

Joe nodded to Chet, and Chet followed him outside. "I thought maybe we'd walk out back," Joe said. "It won't hurt to take a look."

Fields and Baker were staring at the office through the glass. "What a mess!" Fields said. "This is awful."

A narrow alley took the boys to the rear of

Morgan's office. A single dim bulb burned above the back door.

"There's a window," Chet said, "but it doesn't look as if anyone's tried to use it. Maybe they— *Joe, look out!*"

A dark figure suddenly stepped out of the shadows and thrust a pistol at the boys. "Hold it right there, you two! Don't move a step!"

Joe and Chet froze. The man was tall and hollow-cheeked. His hair was cropped close and he wore aviator-style glasses. Joe saw the badge on his shirt and let out a breath.

"I'm Joe Hardy," he explained, "and this is Chet Morton. We came over with the sheriff from the cafe."

The man nodded and holstered his weapon. "Sorry about that. You're the detectives, right? Thought I'd seen you two around. I'm Bob Wilson, Vard's deputy."

"Do you have any idea how the prowler got in?" Chet asked.

"I know exactly how he did it," Wilson said. He pulled a flashlight from his belt and pointed it at the door. He just jimmied the lock with a crowbar and walked in. The locks in this town wouldn't stop a strong rabbit."

"What's that?" Chet asked.

"What?"

"Right there. On the steps."

Deputy Wilson aimed his light at the spot. "Just old yellow mud." He bent and touched the smudge. "Nearly dry, though." He grinned at Chet with approval. "You have a good eye, young man. Only this mud's been here longer than a few minutes. It couldn't belong to our prowler."

"May I borrow your light a minute?" Chet asked. The deputy handed him his light, and Chet held it close to the spot. He dug at the mud with his finger, and held a dab up to the light. "I thought so," he said.

"What's that?" Joe asked. "It looks like ants."

"Termites," Chet corrected. "There must be dozens of dead termites stuck in that mud."

The deputy looked puzzled. "So what? Is that supposed to mean something?"

Chet shrugged. "I don't know. Maybe, maybe not. Bugs are, ah—a kind of hobby of mine," he confided. "I notice things like that."

"Deputy Wilson," Joe asked, "do you have yellow mud like this around here?"

Wilson scratched his head. "No. Lots of it in certain parts of the swamp, though. Like I said, boys—that mud's been here a while. Whoever broke in tonight didn't leave it."

"Since it's not important, you don't mind if I take a sample with me, do you?" Chet asked.

"Take all you like," Deputy Wilson grinned. "One thing we're not going to miss in the Big Thicket is a couple of ounces of mud!"

The Jayhawkers and Rebels' celebration began early in the morning with a parade that started at the square. Joe, Frank and Chet marched with the Confederates behind the band. Marilyn Baker had delivered their uniforms the night before. They were costumed in gray trousers with gold striping down the sides, gray jackets with gold buttons, and billed caps. They carried replicas of Civil War rifles, designed to fire smoke instead of bullets. The Jayhawkers were dressed in a ragtag blend of clothing—baggy cotton pants, overalls, old felt hats, coonskin caps and fringed leather jackets.

"Hey, look," Frank pointed, "over there!" He waved and called out, and Joe and Chet turned their heads. A float was just rounding the courthouse ahead, and riding atop it were a dozen pretty girls in full-skirted "Southern belle" dresses. Bea, Marilyn and E.D. saw the boys and waved back.

"I don't know what Bea and Marilyn have for you guys," Chet grinned, "but E.D. has prepared some fried chicken for after the battle. Fried chicken's one of my favorites!"

"I wonder how she found out?" Frank asked.

Chet frowned. "Are you kidding? I told her, of course. I didn't want her to have to guess!"

Frank and Joe laughed. A few minutes later, the parade moved out of town for the picnic grounds. The Rebel cavalry, twenty boys who'd furnished their own horses, were already lined up under the trees. Past them were the mule-drawn supply wagons that would make up the famous Lost Column. The Jayhawkers exchanged friendly jeers with the Rebels, and marched off to prepare for their attack. Vard Proctor headed the Jayhawker forces, while Deputy Wilson served as "Colonel" of the Confederates.

"All right, now, settle down and listen," Wilson told his small army. The cavalry and infantrymen went silent.

"Yes, sir, Colonel Deputy, sir!" someone shouted from the rear, and everyone laughed.

"Okay," Wilson grinned. "Now, most of you fellas have been to at least one rehearsal. The wagons go past the picnic grounds where everybody will be watching. The enemy attacks and we lose." Someone booed, and Wilson held up a hand. "I don't want anything happening the way it did three years ago, when the Rebels got all excited and won. It just didn't happen that way.

Now, you only have one shot of black powder. Save it for the attack. We want plenty of smoke. Let's go, Rebels!"

The Confederates gave a yell, and followed the wagons through the trees.

"You three are hereby appointed as scouts," Wilson told the three friends. "That means you sneak along the ravine over there on the other side of the column. Watch for Jayhawkers, and when you see 'em, sing out."

"Boy, that sounds like a pretty exciting assignment," Chet said when Wilson was gone.

"Maybe," Frank grinned. "Either that, or he knows we haven't been to any rehearsals, and wants to make sure we don't mess up the battle."

Twenty minutes later, the wagons began to roll. The foot soldiers marched in ragged lines alongside, rifles at the ready. The cavalry led the way with "Colonel" Deputy Wilson out front. Beside him rode a sergeant carrying the flag of the Confederacy, the "stars and bars." The actual battle had been fought deep in the swamp, but the reenactment was held in chest-high grass. The grass helped hide the wagons, and made the column look authentic.

Frank, Joe and Chet crept along a steep-sided gully to the right of the column. Giant oaks shaded the ravine. They could see the other Rebels just above.

"I'll bet the *real* Confederate scouts were farther off," Joe said. "We couldn't give the column more than two seconds warning. If we see anything—that's it!"

"Just keep your eyes open," Chet said dryly. "Maybe you'll win a medal, Joe."

"We're not going to win any medals stuck way down here," Joe told him.

Suddenly, the crowd at the picnic grounds began to cheer. Frank stopped and listened. An instant later, gunfire sounded above. Dark puffs of smoke rose over the grass.

"They've attacked the other side!" Joe cried out. "We're going to miss all the excitement!"

"Let's get up there and join the fun," Frank grinned. "They sure don't need us as scouts anymore."

Slinging the rifle over his shoulder, Frank began climbing the steep side of the ravine, hanging onto exposed roots from the trees above. Joe and Chet followed. They could hear the Rebel and Jayhawker soldiers shouting and firing off their guns.

Halfway to the top, the root Joe was holding onto snapped in two. He gave a shout and slid back down to the bottom.

"Hey, are you all right?" Frank called out.

"I'm fine," Joe yelled back. "But I'm going to miss the whole battle."

"Come on," Chet said, "it's still going strong."

Joe dusted off his hands and searched for a better path to the top. He spotted a good bundle of roots ten yards down the ravine and started for it.

Frank, nearly at the top, paused and glanced back to see how Joe was coming along. His heart nearly stopped. He leaned out and yelled at the top of his lungs.

"Joe, run—get out of there fast!"

Joe looked up and waved. He couldn't hear Frank's warning over the sounds of the battle above. Frank knew it was too late—even if Joe turned and saw the herd of frightened horses thundering toward him in the ravine . . .

10   A Close Call

Grasping the root of the tree in one hand, Frank tore the Civil War rifle from his shoulder, pointed it at the charging horses below and pulled the trigger. The weapon went off with a roar. A shower of sparks and a harmless plume of smoke filled the ravine. The lead horse jerked to a stop, pawed the air and tried to turn away. For an instant, the stampede jammed up behind him.

Joe whirled around and saw the frightened animal towering above him. He let out a yell and leaped frantically up the side of the gully. The runaway herd galloped past him and vanished in a thick cloud of dust.

Joe dropped to the ground and stared up the ravine. "Boy," he said shakily, "that's about as close as I've ever come to getting mashed flat as a pancake. Thanks, Frank!"

Frank and Chet joined Joe down below. Frank squinted narrowly up the ravine. "We'd better find out where those horses came from and notify whoever's in charge — before someone *does* get flattened."

They walked quickly up the ravine under the trees. The sounds of battle died to their left. They could hear the former "enemies" laughing and joking together. A moment later, a boy in a Rebel uniform hurried toward them.

"Listen," he said, pausing to catch his breath, "did you guys see about fifteen horses go by? They must've come this way!"

"I'll say they did," Joe said tightly. "They nearly ran us down. What happened back there?"

"Beats me!" the boy groaned. "But it's going to take the rest of the day to round 'em up!" He broke into a run once more, and disappeared down the ravine.

Thirty yards farther along the gully, they found the spot where the horses had broken free. The ravine ended abruptly against a steep, rocky cliff. The horses had been herded into a makeshift rope corral. Broken strands of rope now lay on the ground, trampled in the dust.

"I hope that fellow gets some help," Joe said. "He's sure going to need it."

"Hey, Frank, Joe—come here and look at this!" Chet exclaimed.

The Hardys turned and saw Chet staring at two pieces of rope clutched in his hands. "You don't have to be much of a detective to figure this one out," he declared.

Frank muttered under his breath, "You're right, Chet. This rope didn't break—it was sliced cleanly in two with a sharp knife."

"Which means it was no accident," Joe finished. "Frank, Chet — someone knew we were in this ravine and deliberately cut those ropes so the horses would stampede straight at us."

"It sure looks that way," Frank agreed.

"We'll never be able to prove it," Chet said. "You can bet that whoever did it is long gone by now."

The boys looked up as voices sounded atop the ravine. Deputy Bob Wilson and several Jayhawker and Rebel troopers ran down the bank and joined them.

"I wondered what had happened to you," Wilson said. He looked curiously at Frank, Joe and

Chet. "I guess you know there are horses runnin' wild all over the place. What are you fellas doing here?"

"We know about the horses," Frank said grimly. He quickly told the lawman what had happened, then showed him the severed ropes.

"No question about it," Wilson frowned. "Someone cut 'em, all right. I don't like what's going on in this town—I don't like it at all." He shook his head at the boys. "I'm sorry. I sent you down in this ravine. You could've all been killed."

"We don't blame you," Joe said. "No one could have guessed this would happen."

"We'll probably never know who did it," Wilson said. "The horses belonged to people who came to watch—folks who like to mount up on celebration day. Everyone knew the animals were here."

Professor Pierce and Harrison Baker were standing together on the picnic grounds. When the boys found them and told their story, Pierce shook his head in dismay.

"It could have been a prank, I suppose, done by someone who didn't realize the harm a bunch of frightened horses could do."

"Martin," Baker said firmly, "the way things

93

are going, I strongly doubt it." He frowned at the three friends. "Rake Morgan talked to us just before the battle. He found out where Zeigler went. Supposedly, he drove to Houston on business."

"Just before Morgan's office was vandalized," Frank noted. "Of course, that doesn't prove a thing. But it sure looks funny, on top of everything else. We—" He stopped, glanced past the others and grinned. "Hey, look who's here. It's Dad!"

Fenton Hardy walked quickly through the trees, greeted Frank, Joe and Chet, and shook hands with Baker and Pierce.

"I got away from Bayport earlier than I'd figured," Mr. Hardy said. "I took the first flight to Houston, rented a car and drove on over." He paused and let his eyes sweep the circle of faces. "I've been an investigator a long time," he said evenly. "From the looks of you people, I'd say plenty's been happening around here."

Frank and Joe exchanged a look. "Dad, it might be easier to tell you what hasn't happened," Frank said, and proceeded to inform his father about the events that had occurred since their arrival.

When Frank was through with his account, Fenton Hardy scratched his chin. "I'll say one thing," he muttered under his breath. "For a man who's gone as far as Zeigler has in this world, he's sure not acting very smart at the moment. He's leaving a trail of circumstantial evidence that's a mile long."

"The only other answer," Frank put in, "is that someone else is trying to make Mr. Zeigler appear guilty."

"Mr. Hardy winked at his son. "That's a real possibility."

"Except for one thing," Joe said. "Who else has a motive? You've always told us a criminal has to have motive and opportunity. If Mr. Zeigler's not behind all this, the case doesn't make sense."

"I'm not saying he's innocent," Mr. Hardy corrected. "I'm saying he's not acting very smart if he's guilty. On the other hand, maybe he's a lot smarter than we think." A sly grin creased the corners of his mouth. "More than once, I've run across criminals who deliberately piled up evidence against themselves—to make the police think they were being framed."

Chet groaned. "Boy, it looks as if we're right back where we started!"

"Maybe, and maybe not," Mr. Hardy said. "I made a call before I left Bayport, and found out something I bet Mr. Zeigler wouldn't want us to

95

know. The Zeigco Corporation's in big financial trouble. Unless this Big Thicket deal goes through, Zeigler could go under."

"This doesn't make sense at all," Baker said. "The more Zeigler threatens Pierce, the more determined *he* is to see Zeigler never gets those rights!"

"You're forgetting one thing," Pierce pointed out. "If I weren't around any more, he could deal with someone else. And I don't think he'd mind that one bit!"

Mr. Hardy nodded. "Well, I suppose we won't be able to solve the case unless we come up with something more helpful than possible motives. There's food all over the place. Why don't we get something to eat?"

Chet's eyes lit up. "I'll go find the girls," he said.

"We'll come with you," Joe volunteered.

Bea, Marilyn and E.D. had gone home to change into jeans. When they came back, they saw the boys looking for them and waved them over to a big-boled oak.

"I'm glad you guys are all right," Marilyn cried out. "Deputy Wilson told us what happened with those horses!"

"I wish we hadn't missed the Battle of the

Lost Column," Joe said. "I sure wanted to see that."

"Sounds to me like you had more excitement than you bargained for," Bea giggled.

"You're right," Joe agreed. "For a second there, I was afraid I was going to miss lunch forever."

The girls laughed. "Well, luckily you didn't," Bea said. "There are barbecued ribs, smoked sausages, and all kinds of other goodies, so dig in."

Chet looked longingly at E.D.'s basket. "And, uh—what's in there, do you suppose?"

"Fried chicken." E.D. grinned. "That's what you wanted, wasn't it?"

"Oh, boy, what a terrific surprise!" Chet said excitedly.

"I hope you can eat it," E.D. told him. "I'm not the world's greatest cook. I don't do a lot of things that most girls do."

"I bet it's great," Chet said. "And I think girls ought to do whatever they like to do."

"So do I," E.D. agreed, "and it's a good thing, too. Bea and Marilyn are always teasing me because my last name's Threader—and I can't sew a thing without stitching up my finger. If Mom hadn't finished my Southern belle dress, I'd have looked like a clown."

"She's right," Marilyn sang out. "E.D. would starve if she had to make a living sewing!"

"But she rides better than any boy in town," Bea added.

"You—you do?" Chet stared at the girl in wonder. "Honest?"

E.D. blushed. "I guess I'm not bad. A couple of those horses that nearly ran Joe down belong to me. We'll go riding sometime if you like."

"That'd be great," Chet said. "I'm a—a pretty good rider myself."

"On what?" Joe grinned. "A bus?"

"Hey, I've been on a horse before!" Chet protested.

"I know." Joe said dryly. "Let me know before you get on one again. I want to get in front of a stampede where it's safe."

11 The Black Mask

The sun was beginning to set when Frank, Joe and Chet helped the girls gather up the remains of the picnic supper.

"Boy, this basket's a lot lighter than when I started," E.D. grinned.

"You don't have to worry about leftovers when Chet's around," Joe told her. "He eats everything but the forks."

"Oh, yeah?" Chet retorted. "I don't see a whole lot of food on your plate, fella."

"That's telling him," Bea laughed. "Joe finished off *everything* I brought. And I think he's still hungry."

"No way," Joe groaned, patting his stomach.

Chet groaned also. "I'm not going to eat for a whole week!"

"Dad and Professor Pierce and Mr. Baker are over by the cars. We can get a ride if we want," Frank reported, pointing to the parking lot.

"Great," Marilyn said. "I need to get back. I have some things to do."

"You two better come with us," Joe grinned at E.D. and Bea. "Chet's going to treat us all to dessert at Pop's Malt Shop."

"Huh?" Chet blinked at Joe. "Did I say that?" Then, after barely a moment's thought, Chet agreed that a visit to Pop's was a good idea.

"So much for not eating for a week," Frank said wryly.

"I don't think I can handle dessert just yet," Marilyn laughed. "And even the *small* servings at Pop's are enough for three people."

"They won't make any money off Joe and Chet," Frank assured her. "Those two—uh-oh, here comes trouble again."

Lew Hawks and Shiner Black were standing under a tree on the path. Both were dressed in Jayhawker costumes. Frank was almost certain the pair were deliberately waiting for them to pass.

"Well, now, if it isn't one of the Rebels from

the big stampede," Hawks said. He gave Frank a crooked grin. "Sure glad you guys weren't *hurt* or anything."

Shiner Black laughed at his friend's joke.

"I bet you are," Frank said tightly. He stood his ground and looked straight in the bully's eyes. "Is that it, or did you have something else to say?"

Shiner looked offended. "This guy's not very friendly, is he, Lew?"

"He sure isn't," Lew said. "I think I'm gonna cry."

"Come on, let's go, Marilyn," Frank said.

Lew took a step to his left and blocked Frank's path. "Sorry," he grinned slyly, "guess you'll have to go around."

"I'm not looking for trouble," Frank told him. "But if—"

"Well, maybe you've got it," Lew said narrowly, "whether you want it or not!" He swung at Frank without warning. Frank ducked and let the fist graze his shoulder. Then, twisting on his heels, he gripped the other boy's arm and flipped him off the side of his hip. Hawks bellowed in surprise and sprawled flat on his back. Frank turned quickly. Shiner Black was starting to spring. He took one look at his friend and changed his mind.

Frank glanced down at Hawks. "Okay if I pass now?"

Hawks pulled himself erect. "I'll get you for this," he growled. "You wait and see if I don't!"

Frank didn't answer. He guided Marilyn down the pathway to the cars.

"Wow," Marilyn exclaimed, "where'd you learn to do that!"

"It's just a basic self-defense move," Frank explained. "They taught us a few karate techniques in gym after school." He smiled and shook his head. "Now, I'm real glad I hung around for the class."

"He meant it, you know," Marilyn said flatly. "Shiner just does what he's told, but Lew's really mean!"

"I'm sure you're right," Frank said. "Bullies can't afford to let anyone get the best of them."

"Be careful," Marilyn warned. "He's not going to get that close to you again. Next time, you won't see him coming."

"Harrison, Martin and I had some time to talk at the picnic," Fenton Hardy told Frank later that evening. "We've come up with a few things, and I'd like to see how they sound to you."

"Fine," Frank said. "We could sure use some ideas."

They were all gathered on the screened-in porch at Harrison Baker's home. Lightning bugs winked through the darkness outside, and locusts droned in the trees.

"We were trying to outguess our unseen enemy," Mr. Hardy said. "Trying to figure what he plans to pull next."

"He's been pretty slick so far," Frank declared. "Whoever he is, he's a step or two ahead all the way."

"I don't know why you say 'whoever,'" Pierce said tightly. "And you, too, Fenton. 'Unseen enemy'—hah! I've seen him, and his name's Nelson Zeigler!"

"I won't say you're wrong," Mr. Hardy told him. "He's our number one suspect, for certain. Still, I have to stick to the rules of a good investigator. And the fact is, we couldn't have Zeigler arrested for jaywalking. We have some pretty solid suspicions and a lot of circumstantial evidence. And that's all."

"In other words," Baker said wryly, "as long as he doesn't get caught, he can do whatever he likes."

"That's the law," Fenton Hardy said. "It sometimes protects the guilty. But it has to be that way to protect the innocent. Fortunately, we have to prove it when someone has committed a crime."

"I know," Pierce sighed. "I'm just on edge, Fenton."

"Getting back to what Dad was saying," Frank put in, "I think I know what he means. It's high time we beat this guy to the punch."

"And how are we going to do that?" Baker asked.

"He seems to know a lot about us," Frank pointed out. "Maybe we can use that to catch him. Set a trap of some kind."

"Frank's right," Mr. Hardy agreed. "If we sit around hoping to surprise him in the act—" He stopped and stared out at the dark. "If it is really Zeigler we're after, we need to know more about him. What about this Turner Fields? From what you two tell me, he's a pretty reasonable person. He's interested in conservation, and he certainly knows Zeigler. Do you think he'd help us?"

"Maybe," the professor said. "But we'd have to be careful. He still has some loyalty to Zeigler, in spite of the fact the man fired him."

Marilyn suddenly stood up. "I think I'll go get us some ice cream now, if it's okay. There's no breeze out, and we could use something cool."

"Good idea," her father grinned.

"Maybe I'd better come along," Frank suggested.

"Just sit still," Marilyn said firmly. "I'll be fine." Baker tossed his daughter the keys to the car. "I don't hear any favorite flavors." She smiled. "That means you *all* get chocolate."

The men laughed and Marilyn disappeared.

Frank turned to his father. "I think you're right about Mr. Fields, Dad. But I agree with the professor. Even though Nelson Zeigler fired him, Fields won't help us unless he's convinced his former boss is guilty."

"And I'm sure he still thinks Zeigler's innocent," Baker added.

"Yes, but he knows Nelson will do almost anything to get his way," Pierce said harshly.

"Zeigler's hard-headed," Frank sighed, "and he's got a temper that won't quit."

"We can't send him to jail for that," Mr. Hardy pointed out. "If having a short fuse is a crime, half the people in the—" His words were lost as a sudden, piercing scream came from outside.

Harrison Baker went white. "Th—that's Marilyn!" he blurted.

Frank was already on his feet, dashing from

the porch through the hall. He yanked open the door and rushed out into the dark. "Marilyn," he shouted, "where are you!"

"*Frank—help me!*" she called out. "Fra—!" Her voice stopped abruptly, as if someone had clamped a strong hand over her mouth. Frank tore through the trees in the direction of her voice.

An engine suddenly roared to life to Frank's left. He saw light from the street shimmer off the top of a car. It had been hidden in the dense undergrowth between Harrison Baker's yard and the house next door. Now it veered in a tight circle, tires whining against the earth. A shower of dirt and small stones stung Frank on his arms and chest. He jumped back as the car skidded completely around and headed for the street. Frank reached through the open window for the dark, masked figure bent over the wheel.

The driver yelled and lashed out with one arm. Frank held on with all his might. His feet dragged the ground as the car raced crazily through the trees. He heard Marilyn's muffled cry and he tore at the driver's arm.

"Jump, Marilyn," he shouted hoarsely. "Do it now!"

The far door burst open and Marilyn vanished into the dark. The masked driver jerked the wheel to the left. Frank saw a big oak coming at him and desperately leaped away. The car roared through the brush, sparked metal at the curb, and screeched onto the street away from the square.

Frank raced back and helped Marilyn to her feet. "Are you all right?" he asked anxiously.

The girl leaned unsteadily against a tree. "I'm going to have some bruises in the morning, and I'm scared right out of my wits. Other than that I'm—I'm just fine . ."

Three men suddenly broke through the brush. "Marilyn," Baker cried out, "are you all right?" He held his daughter against him.

"I'm okay," Marilyn said weakly, "thanks to Frank."

"What happened?" Fenton Hardy said tightly. "Who was it, son? Could you tell?"

Frank shook his head. "His face was covered, Dad. Black ski mask. I couldn't tell much about the car, either. If it had any plates, I didn't see them." He looked squarely at his father. "Whatever this guy's up to, he doesn't care who gets hurt. We'd better stop him, and stop him fast!"

12 *Firebug!*

"Tell me exactly what happened," Frank said to Marilyn. "Everything—from the moment you left the porch."

They were walking back to the house through the trees. Pierce and Harrison Baker had run ahead to call the sheriff. Fenton Hardy remained behind to study the spot where the man in the mask had parked his car.

"Our car was in the driveway," Marilyn explained. "I wouldn't have even seen the man if I hadn't decided to walk around the house and check the gate. Mom keeps it closed because deer sometimes get in and eat from the garden."

"And that's where you saw him?"

"Well, actually I didn't. He saw me!" Marilyn

shuddered at the thought. "He came out of nowhere, put his hand over my mouth, and dragged me off." She gave Frank a wide-eyed stare. "Why? What did he want with me, Frank?"

"My guess is he assumed you saw him and he wanted to keep you quiet, make a clean getaway, and set you free out of town," Frank said. "I knew I should have gone with you to get that ice cream."

"I don't even feel like ice cream any more." Marilyn groaned.

Frank turned as his father came into view through the trees. "Find anything, Dad?" he asked.

"Maybe," Mr. Hardy replied. "I need to talk to you a minute."

"I'll go on inside," Marilyn told him. "See you later."

"You *did* find something," Frank said to his father. "I can tell."

"Guess you know me pretty well," Fenton Hardy muttered. He flicked on his flashlight and held up a small object. Frank examined it closely.

"It's electrical wire," he said curiously. "Pretty small, too. It could have come from anywhere, only—"

"Only it didn't, right?" Mr. Hardy suggested.

"No. The copper wire inside the insulation is still bright. I'd say it was freshly snipped."

"Unless I'm wrong," Mr. Hardy said, "our masked intruder stood beside his car and cut this wire before he sneaked up to Baker's house."

Frank told his father where Marilyn had surprised the man. "He was coming from behind the house. What do you suppose he was doing—just listening to us, or what?"

"Maybe," Fenton Hardy said tightly. "Maybe that and something more. Come on — we're going to find out right now."

They searched the rear wall of the house, concentrating on the area near the screened-in porch. Frank found a thin, almost invisible wire leading to the ground from a point just below the windowsill. The microphone at the end of the wire was no larger than the head of a nail.

Mr. Hardy traced the wire to the ground, then reached under the house and retrieved a small metal box the size of a bar of soap. A low whistle escaped his lips. He replaced the box where he'd found it, and motioned Frank away.

"Go in and tell Pierce we'll meet him back at his house. If we wait until the sheriff arrives, we'll be stuck here answering questions. I want to get to Pierce's place fast! It may be wired, too!"

An hour later, Frank, Joe, Chet and Mr. Hardy sat together in the boys' second-story bedroom.

"Dad," Joe asked, after Frank and Mr. Hardy had told their story, "the 'bug' you found outside the professor's study downstairs—it's just like the one near Mr. Baker's back porch?"

"Exactly," Fenton Hardy nodded. "I'm sure our man went right from here to Baker's place."

"He used pretty sophisticated equipment," Frank said. "The mike is small but supersensitive, and the mini-tape recorder and transmitter is voice activated. It only starts up if someone's talking."

"Which means whoever placed the two recorders doesn't ever have to risk coming near them again," Joe finished. "He can send an electronic signal from wherever he wants, activate the tape, and see if anything's on it."

Mr. Hardy nodded. "He won't have to come much closer than a mile."

"We'll never catch him now," Chet groaned. "He can just—" He stopped, and his face suddenly creased in a grin. "Hey, that's it, isn't it? That's why you left those bugs where they were.

We're going to set a trap for him, right?"

"If we can," Frank grinned.

"It's just like fishing," Joe said. "All we have to do is find the right bait."

Mr. Hardy stood up. "For the time being, let's keep this to ourselves. I would like to confide in Pierce and Baker, but they're both on edge as it is. If they knew someone was listening to every word they said . . ."

"You're right," Frank agreed.

Fenton Hardy yawned. "We'd all better get some sleep." He glanced at Joe and grinned. "As you said, son, we need to go digging for bait . . ."

The closing ceremonies of the Jayhawkers and Rebels' celebration began at ten the next morning a few blocks from the square. Chet went with Mr. Hardy and Professor Pierce. Frank and Joe decided to look once more at the spot where the prowler had parked his car.

Before they left the house, Rake Morgan called with two bits of news. Nelson Zeigler was back in town at the Lansdale Hotel. Vard Proctor had found the prowler's car, deserted on a logging road to the north. It had been stolen, and so far they'd found no fingerprints or clues.

"Dad's right," Joe said fiercely. "The only way we're going to catch this guy is to play his own game. I bet we *can* trap him with those tape recorders."

"It'll have to be a pretty good plan," Frank said, "something that will work the first time. We won't get a second chance."

"Hey—where are you boys headed?" a voice called out behind them. Frank and Joe turned to see Harrison Baker coming toward them across the square. He caught up to them and smiled at the pair. "I got tired of the celebration. Too many speeches."

"We want to take another look at the place where the prowler parked," Joe explained.

"Good idea," Baker nodded. "Proctor's men were all over it this morning, but you never can tell. I'll be home if you need me. Oh—there's Turner Fields."

Nelson Zeigler's former employee waved from the front of the cafe and walked up to greet them. "I'm glad I ran into you," he said. "I've got something you'd better hear."

"Fine," Baker told him. "We can sit on my porch if you like."

Fields looked embarrassed. "Uh, would you mind if we talked in the cafe? To tell you the truth, I left Houston early this morning, and didn't stop for breakfast."

"Sure," Baker agreed with a grin. "The Armadillo Cafe's my second home, anyway. Since I live next door, they get worried if I don't show up at least once a day."

Fields led them to a table and ordered breakfast. When the waiter left, he looked at his hands and frowned. "I don't know how to say this, but I'd better just start. I drove to Houston for a reason. I — still feel loyal to Mr. Zeigler, even though he fired me. But I have to do what I think is right." He paused, quickly, looked at Frank and Joe, then let his eyes rest on Baker. "I don't know whether you know this, but the Zeigco Corporation's in trouble. Money trouble."

"We'd heard about that," Joe admitted.

"Good, good." Baker looked relieved. "Then I don't have to feel like a — a traitor, by telling you."

"I don't think anyone would call you that, sir," Frank put in.

"I heard about what happened last night," Fields went on. "That terrible business with your daughter, Harrison. She's all right, isn't she?"

"She's fine, although I don't think she slept too well last night."

Fields nervously ran a hand through his hair. "I can't believe Zeigler would go this far to get his way," he said wearily. "I just can't—"

Suddenly, a loud explosion rocked the cafe. Glasses rattled, and a startled waiter dropped his tray.

"Wha—what on earth was that?" Baker cried out.

"Come on," Fields snapped. "Let's get out of here!"

At that moment, the door to the kitchen flew open. A wide-eyed cook ran into the dining room. "Fire, fire!" she shrieked. "Everybody run—hurry!"

Frank and Joe quickly followed the other customers outside. Black plumes of smoke rose up to the sky. A solid sheet of flames licked at the side of the building.

"No!" Baker gasped, "It—it's got my house, too!"

The side of Baker's house was less than ten feet from the cafe. The walls were charred black, and as Frank and Joe watched, a window exploded from the heat.

"That's my library," Baker shouted hoarsely. "All my papers—my work!"

Turner Fields grasped his arm. "Harrison, the fire department will be here any minute. It's all right. They'll—Harrison, don't!"

Before Turner Fields could stop him, Baker broke loose and ran for his house. Fields started after him, Frank and Joe at his heels. A fire engine wailed coming around the square. Baker and Fields vanished. An instant later, Fields appeared again, guiding Baker through a thick cloud of smoke. Baker coughed and wiped his eyes.

"My work . . . all my work," he moaned.

"Sir, please," Joe said, "we've got to get out of the yard!"

Baker looked stunned as firemen swept past him with their hoses.

"They got here pretty fast," Fields assured him. "I'm certain they can save a great deal."

Frank exchanged a look with his brother. Both of them knew the fire had spread too fast, with too much heat, to leave anything at all unscathed in the historian's study.

13 The Mysterious Voice

The firemen set up fans to clear the smoke from Harrison Baker's house. As soon as there was fresh air to breathe, Baker was inside, rummaging through the ruins of his study.

"Look at this," he moaned. "Everything's gone—there's nothing left at all!" He picked through a pile of soggy ashes, let out a sigh and stood up. "It's no use. One shelf of books can be salvaged, but my own historical research, that's gone for good."

Marilyn put her arms around her father. "I know it's awful," she said, "but I guess we're lucky we didn't lose the whole house, Dad."

"Yes, yes, you're right." Baker forced a painful

smile. "I suppose I should be grateful, and I am —but all that work!"

"I don't suppose the material can be replaced can it, sir?" Joe asked.

Baker shook his head. "A lot of my own notes and research can be written again from memory, given time. What cannot be replaced are the valuable documents and old letters I've collected on the history of the Big Thicket. Those records of the past are gone forever!"

Joe and Frank met their father and Chet Morton outside. After inspecting the ruins of Baker's study, Mr. Hardy had joined Fire Chief Billy Wallace and Sheriff Proctor in the rear of the Armadillo Cafe.

"There'll be an investigation," Mr. Hardy reported, "but as near as the chief can tell, a gas leak started the fire. Fumes built up and something sparked the explosion."

"It spread so quickly," Frank said. "The flames had leaped to Mr. Baker's house by the time we ran outside."

Rake Morgan walked up with Turner Fields. "We're real lucky no one was hurt," Morgan remarked. "It sure could've been a lot worse."

"If it hadn't been for Mr. Fields, here," Joe said, "Mr. Baker might have been trapped inside his house."

"Nonsense," Fields scoffed. "You boys would

have stopped him if I hadn't been there."

"But you *were* there," Morgan said firmly. He grinned at Turner Fields. "Since you're looking for a new job, maybe you'll consider moving to Black Cypress Creek. The town would be proud to have you."

"Don't think I haven't thought about it," Fields said. He looked past the square at the old courthouse. "This would be a real fine place to live, if you ask me."

Fenton Hardy made several calls, then told the boys late in the afternoon that he'd be driving out of town and coming back the next morning.

"I know Dad," Joe said when he was gone. "When he doesn't say exactly where he's headed, that means he's onto something."

"You're right," Frank agreed. He slipped into a clean shirt and combed his hair. "We'll find out what it is when he gets back. Are you ready, Joe? We're supposed to meet the girls at Pop's Malt Shop by seven-thirty."

The phone rang downstairs, and someone picked it up at once.

"I'll be ready in a minute," Joe growled. "I think Chet borrowed my last pair of clean socks. I can't find them anywhere."

At that moment, someone bounded quickly up

the stairs. Both boys turned as Chet burst into the room.

"Frank, Joe—" Chet swallowed hard and tried to speak.

"Hey, what's wrong?" Frank asked.

"That—phone call," Chet said tightly. "A man asked who I was, and I told him. He—he said if we wanted information about what's happening in the Thicket, we'd better be at Moccasin Point on Willow Creek at nine in the morning. We have to take a boat and come alone, he said. He doesn't want the police involved."

Frank's eyes narrowed. "Did you recognize his voice?"

"No—he talked in a kind of—throaty whisper."

"Whoever this guy is," Joe said soberly, "he must think we're pretty dumb. We'd be walking right into a trap!"

"You're probably right," Frank said. "Chet, where's Professor Pierce?"

"In the kitchen. I think he's fixing something special for supper."

Frank frowned in thought. "Let's talk to him in there, then. We don't want to get near that bug that's tuned into his study."

Five minutes later, the Hardys were consulting with their host.

Pierce looked up from the map he'd spread on the kitchen table. "Right there," he said, tapping a spot with his finger. "That's Willow Creek and there's Moccasin Point." His face clouded with concern. "If it's a trap, your mysterious caller couldn't have picked a better place. Willow Creek's a narrow channel through the swamp—choked on both sides with heavy growth, and scarcely six feet wide. An army could hide in there waiting for you to pass and you'd never see a soul."

"What about this Moccasin Point?" Joe asked. "It looks as if Willow Creek widens into a lake right there."

"It does," Pierce told him. "But you have to pass through the narrows to get there."

"I see what you're trying to say," Frank said grimly. "Our caller wants us to think he's going to meet us at Moccasin Point, out in the open . . ."

"Only he'll be waiting for us somewhere along the way," Chet finished.

"Exactly," Pierce said firmly. "It's too great a risk, boys. I think we'd better leave this one up to the sheriff. Let him catch this fellow and ask him a few questions."

Joe shook his head. "Whoever he is, he's too smart to let that happen. It's not hard to keep an eye on the sheriff's office and two or three patrol cars. Any unusual activity would tip off our caller and send him running."

"Hm, I'm afraid you're right," Pierce agreed. "Still, we don't have much choice."

"Wait—wait a minute," Frank muttered under his breath. "If this is a trap, our caller would wait for us somewhere along here—right, professor?" He ran a finger down a section of Willow Creek.

"Yes," Pierce told him. "The dangerous spot is this stretch about sixty, seventy yards long, where the creek narrows before it reaches open water at Moccasin Point."

Chet glanced curiously at Frank. "You've got an idea, I can tell."

"Maybe," Frank said. "Look—this guy'll probably be waiting for us, hidden in a boat among the willows. We'd be crazy to run our boat right into his trap. But look here—about a quarter of a mile to the north, just south of Moccasin Point, there's a small road that runs past Willow Creek. We could take your boat, professor, and launch it quietly into the lake. I'd guess there are plenty of reeds and grasses to give us cover."

"Yes, yes, there are," Pierce said thoughtfully.

"I get it," Joe exclaimed. "He's waiting for us to pass—and we're already beyond him!"

"From the looks of this map," Chet said, "we could watch the narrows of Willow Creek without giving ourselves away."

"When he gets tired of waiting," Frank said, "he'll come out. Then we follow and see where he goes. If we're lucky, we'll find out who he is."

"If he says he'll meet you at nine," Pierce noted, "you can bet he'll be there before that."

"By seven, I'd guess," Frank said. "He wouldn't want to fight the mosquitoes much longer than that. I think we'd better get there by five."

"I'm calling the girls to tell them we won't be going to Pop's tonight," Joe groaned. "Morning isn't that far off when you're getting up at three or four."

Pierce frowned and ran a hand over his jaw. "I don't like it," he said darkly. "It's a good plan, but there's still some risk involved."

"We'll be all right," Frank assured him. "We'll see him before he sees us."

Pierce stood, glanced at the map, then looked squarely at the three friends. "Remember," he warned, "the last people you met out on the lake were blasting away with a shotgun."

"We're not likely to forget," Joe said dryly.

Long before sunup, the flat-bottomed aluminum boat was well hidden in a thick stand of reeds near the shore of the lake. It was Joe's turn to watch. Frank and Chet dozed in the stern under a veil of mosquito netting. Joe paused to rub more repellent on his face and hands, then peered through the brush. To his left was Moccasin Point, a narrow stretch of marshy ground across the water. Straight ahead, he could see the spot where Willow Creek flowed sluggishly into the lake. The early morning sun had already turned the Thicket into a furnace.

Joe started as a swamp rabbit broke cover on the bank and darted away. Far past the marsh, a bull alligator gave a deep, throaty call.

The boat rocked slightly and Frank crawled up beside his brother. "See anything?" he asked.

"Nothing," Joe said. He squinted at his watch and frowned. "I don't like this, Frank. It's after eight now. If there's an ambusher out there, we should have seen him come up the creek and hide his boat. He couldn't have gotten here any earlier than we did!"

"Maybe we guessed wrong," Frank said. "Maybe our mysterious caller really does want to give us information. Maybe he'll just show up on Moccasin Point as he said."

Joe gave his brother a skeptical frown. "I don't believe that and neither do you. He's here,

Frank—and he's not any friend. The only thing I can figure is he *didn't* come up the narrows as we thought. Maybe there's another channel that leads into Willow Creek."

Frank waved a cloud of mosquitoes away. "That's got to be it. Professor Pierce warned us, remember? Every little stream in the Thicket's not on the map. And the land and water shift all the time."

"Right," Joe said, "which means we could—" His mouth suddenly went slack. He clutched Frank's arm and pointed frantically to the left. Frank took one quick look and shoved his brother flat against the bottom of the boat.

The mysterious caller wasn't waiting in Willow Creek. He was gliding silently toward them through the reeds, not twenty yards away!

14 Swamp Chase

Frank held his breath as the boat drew nearer. It was too late to move, too late to do anything at all. He could hear the bow brushing dry reeds aside. An oar swept lightly through the water. He looked at his brother beside him. Joe's eyes were following the shadowy outline of the boat which was drawing closer every second.

Frank knew at once what had happened. The mysterious caller had come from the *north* end of the lake—he hadn't come through Willow Creek at all. *How, though?* Frank wondered. *Was there a secret channel that didn't show on the map?*

Joe gripped Frank's arm. The older Hardy felt his heart beating wildly against his chest. A dark shadow passed behind the reeds not two feet away. Frank saw the side of the boat, the blur of a man's shoulders. An oar pushed reeds aside, missing their own craft by inches. Frank let out a breath as the sounds grew farther away.

"He missed us," Joe whispered. "He didn't see us at all!"

"Quiet," Frank warned. "Don't move. Let him get closer to the creek." He raised himself up cautiously and peered through the reeds. The boat was a good twenty yards away in open water, moving along the fringes of the lake. Frank swallowed hard when he saw that its occupant wore a black ski mask! It appeared to be the same man who'd tried to carry Marilyn off in his car!

"What's he doing?" Joe whispered. "Where is he?"

"He's headed for the mouth of Willow Creek," Frank said. "He sure is late getting here. I wonder what kept him?"

Joe rolled his eyes. "Who cares? Frank—he missed seeing us by a *foot*! This is sure our lucky—"

Suddenly, Chet sat up straight in the stern of the boat, threw his mosquito netting aside, and yawned. "Hey, you guys, what's going on?" he called out. "What time is it?"

Frank and Joe stared. They suddenly realized

Chet had slept through the last fifteen minutes and was not even aware of the suspect!

"Quiet!" Joe whispered harshly. "Get down!"

"Huh?" Chet looked puzzled.

The loud roar of an outboard motor broke the silence.

"Uh-oh," Frank groaned, "he heard us! He's turning back! Joe, Chet—start that motor up, fast. We've got to get out of here!"

Joe scrambled to the stern of the boat. He pressed the starter and the outboard sputtered.

Frank's heart sank. "What is it? What's wrong?"

"I don't know," Joe said tightly. "It won't work. Sounds like it's flooded."

"It can't be," Frank shouted. Keep trying!" He poked his head over the reeds. The man in the mask was cutting through the water, heading straight for them.

"Here—let me look at that," Chet said soberly. He snapped up the aluminum cover and worked furiously on the motor. Finally, he snapped the cover shut. "Okay. Try it again."

Joe pressed the starter once more. The motor coughed and died.

"Again!" Chet snapped.

Joe took a deep breath. The motor sputtered, threatened to quit, then suddenly roared into life. "Here we go," Joe cried out. "Hang on, you guys!"

He flipped the throttle on full. Water churned in a froth and the boat leaped ahead, tearing through the reeds. In an instant, the marshy shoreline fell away behind the stern.

"Yaaaaaah, *look out!*" Chet shouted. The other boat thundered across their bow, nearly swamping them in its wake.

"Keep going," Frank shouted. "Don't stop!" Glancing over his shoulder, he saw the masked man's boat turn quickly and come after them again. Joe headed across the lake past Moccasin Point at full speed. But the boat behind them rapidly closed the gap. Its motor was much bigger and it was carrying only one man.

"He's too fast," Frank shouted. "We can't beat him in open water!"

Joe nodded in understanding. He turned the boat sharply to starboard, ripping through a stand of willows only inches from the shore. For a moment, they were lost in a curtain of green. Joe turned again, this time to port. Just ahead, a forest of thick-boled cypress trees rose out of the dark water.

"He's coming," Chet warned. "He's right on our tail."

"Let's see how he likes getting dizzy," Joe

said tightly. "That big motor won't help him in here. Hang on, everybody!"

He guided the boat on a fast, twisting path through the maze of trees. The water was no more than a foot deep, and Frank cringed as the sharp tips of stumps and sunken logs flashed by.

"Joe," he yelled out, "if you hit one of those, it'll tear out the bottom of the boat!"

"I know," Joe called back. "What do you want me to *do*!"

Frank didn't answer. He held on tight and tried not to look. The masked pursuer stayed with them, veering through the trees in their wake. Frank glanced ahead. The watery forest gave way to a sea of swampy grass. Joe turned sharply to port. He knew the spot was too shallow and headed for open water.

"Joe—he's cutting us off," snapped Chet. "Hurry!"

Too late, Joe realized he had made a mistake. The man behind them knew the lake, saw them headed for the shallows, and moved to stop them. His faster, more powerful boat was driving them into the shore.

"Hold on," Joe warned. "We're not going to make it—!"

The boys' boat plunged ahead, straight for the tangle of grass. For a moment, their speed kept them going. Then, suddenly, the craft's metal bottom hit mud and jerked abruptly to a stop. The motor choked and died, burying its props in heavy silt.

"Come on," Joe said, "let's get out of here!" He jumped in the water and slogged to shore. The bank was still twenty feet away. None of the three looked back until they were hidden in a thick growth of tupelo and green palmetto fans.

The man in the mask had slowed his motor to a crawl. He cruised beyond the weeds, searching the shore where the boys had disappeared.

"What do you think he's going to do?" Chet asked.

"I don't know," Joe replied. "What I'm wondering now is what we're going to do. If I remember that map, this side of the lake goes right into the swamp for miles. Without a pirogue we're stuck. And there's no way we can get back to the car without swimming."

"Forget it," Chet said darkly. "There are alligators out there. I heard them."

"We don't have a choice," Frank sighed. "We're going to have to head away from the lake and try to find a way out. If that guy decides to land somewhere and follow us on foot . . ."

"Yes," Chet finished, "he knows this place a lot better than we do." He looked curiously at

Frank and Joe. "Did either of you see if he had a—a shotgun?"

Joe shook his head. "I didn't see one, but that doesn't mean it wasn't there. . ."

"Joe, Chet—" Frank suddenly pointed through the brush. "He's taking off, heading around Moccasin Point."

"There's dry land over there," Joe said grimly. "I knew it! He's coming after us, Frank."

"Maybe," Frank said. "We sure can't wait and find out. Come on—the quicker we get out of here, the better."

"Great," Chet muttered. "Which way is *out*?"

Frank glanced at his watch and saw they'd been walking nearly an hour. It seemed longer than that. The way ahead was getting rougher every moment. At times, the narrow stretch of dry land completely disappeared. They had to wade through stagnant water clotted with weeds, hoping for the next soggy patch of solid ground. Tall cypress trees blotted out the sun. Mosquitoes attacked them in clouds, and the air was too thick to breathe.

Frank stopped as Joe suddenly turned and excitedly motioned him forward. Frank made his way through shallow water, and Chet reached out to help him through a tangle of vines. A few feet away, a cottonmouth moccasin slithered away atop the water.

"Up here," Joe said in a half whisper, "the ground gets higher past the trees. And someone has *been* here. Not long ago, either." He pushed a veil of moss aside and pointed down to the narrow strip of land.

Frank went to his knees. There were footprints and the gray ashes of a fire. Charred bits of wood were still warm.

"There's garbage over here in the brush," Chet reported. "Tin cans and stuff."

"Hey, what's this?" Frank scraped powdery ash aside and pulled out several scraps of paper. The edges were burned, but he could still read the words clearly. He stared at them a moment, then suddenly jerked to his feet.

"Hey, you two, look at this!" he exclaimed, and Joe and Chet crowded in to see.

"That one's part of a map," Chet said. "Uh, *'south something-something creek . . . two miles due east of . . .'* I can't decipher the rest."

"Listen to this." Frank read from the other scrap. " '*—federate order . . . this day . . .*' That *federate* part has to be Confederate, right? *'Proceed to . . . shipment numbers 7110 . . . 7111.'* " He paused and looked up at Joe and Chet. "Do you notice the handwriting on this—and on the piece of the map, too? It's in an old-fashioned script, and the ink's brown and faded. These papers are *old*, historical documents like—"

"Like the ones from Mr. Baker's study," Chet finished. He frowned "But—that doesn't make sense, does it? All those papers were burned up in the fire. How could someone have burned them here?"

"He couldn't," Frank said, "Unless—" His eyes suddenly went wide. "Unless someone stole them from Baker's house before the fire and brought them out here in the swamp."

"Why would anyone want to do that?" Joe asked.

"I don't know," Frank admitted, "but it looks as if that's what happened. There's no other way those papers could ha—*Chet, Joe*—look out!"

Chet and Joe sprang to their feet as something crashed through the brush just behind them. An arm suddenly appeared, tore a tangle of vines aside, and the man in the black ski mask came bounding straight for them!

15   A Puzzling Clue

For an instant, Chet and Joe froze. Then, both boys broke into a run, tearing through a stand of young willows. The man stopped, turned around, and came at Frank. Scarcely pausing to think, Frank scooped a handful of ash in his face. The man bellowed and flailed at his eyes. Frank ran past him not daring to look back. Tangled vines tore at his clothes. Chet and Joe were nowhere in sight. He could hear the man behind him, crashing through the brush.

"Frank, *Frank!*"

A moment later, Frank spotted Chet and Joe ahead of him. They frantically waved him on from a thick stand of pine. He risked a look over his shoulder. The man in the mask was right behind him and gaining fast.

"Keep going," the young detective shouted to his friends. "Don't stop!"

Chet and Joe ran, Frank directly at their heels. The way ahead was clear. A narrow, sandy path twisted through the thick green vegetation. If the path didn't end, Frank knew they had a chance. If it suddenly dropped off into the swamp, they were trapped. They'd never outrun their pursuer through the muddy, shallow water and the—

Suddenly, Chet and Joe yelled, turned on their heels and ran back in Frank's direction. Frank stared, then heard a low, throaty growl. A moment later he saw several big razorback hogs charging straight down the path at his companions!

"Jump," he cried." "Get out of the way!" He dove for cover as five or six shaggy forms hurtled by, allowing him a glimpse of yellow tusks and red eyes, and of hair standing stiff on bristly backs.

Chet landed heavily on Frank. They heard their pursuer cry out as the razorbacks drove straight for him. Frank came to his feet in time to see the man running as fast as he could, the big animals dangerously close behind.

Joe appeared from the other side of the path.

"You guys all right?" he said shakily. "Wow, I think we disturbed a whole family of those uglies!"

"Come on," Frank said, "now's our chance. Let's get out of here while we can."

Chet and Joe needed no encouragement. The three companions moved quickly through the trees, alert for any sounds of pursuit.

"Uh-oh," Joe said suddenly, this is the end of the line."

The grove of trees ended abruptly and they were facing the swamp again. There was no dry land for a hundred yards or more.

"Look," Chet said, pointing at the ground, "those razorbacks came across here. That means it's safe for us, too."

"Right," Frank said, "let's go!"

The black water was ankle deep, and for a change the bottom was sand instead of mud. They were halfway across when the high-pitched sound of a motor reached their ears.

"Oh, no!" Chet's jaw fell. "He's got his boat and he's coming back!"

"Wait," Frank cautioned. "That's not an outboard Chet, it's something else."

Suddenly, a strange craft moved swiftly around the bend to their right. It was a broad, flat-bottom boat with a powerful propeller nearly five feet high near the stern. The prop was inside a mesh cage, and looked like a giant electric fan.

"It's a swamp boat," Joe exclaimed. "And — hey, look, it's Dad! The professor and Deputy Wilson are with him!"

The boys waved as the boat whirred noisily over to meet them. Fenton Hardy reached out to help the three aboard.

"Boy, are we glad to see you," Joe grinned. "We were afraid you were someone else!"

Pierce cut the engine and the giant fan whined to a stop.

"Now we can hear ourselves think," Mr. Hardy said. "Martin said you boys might be in trouble. From the looks of you, I'd say he guessed right."

"We were in *big* trouble," Frank sighed, "until we got some unexpected help." He quickly explained what had happened since the man in the ski mask had spotted them across the lake. For the moment, he left out the part about finding scraps of Hamilton Baker's papers.

When he was through, Mr. Hardy frowned and let out a breath. "It sounds to me like you got off lucky. Whoever that fellow is, he really means business."

"If those hogs caught up with him," Deputy Wilson said grimly, "he'll be hurt bad — or maybe something worse. But if he got to his boat, there's no use trying to catch him. I'm going to have to find out what happened."

"While we're at it," Mr. Hardy said, "I'd like to take a look at that campsite you boys found."

Deputy Wilson started the big fan. Moments later, they circled back to the dry strip of land where the boys had been surprised by their pursuer. Once ashore, it was clear the man had escaped. His tracks led back into the water, and Professor Pierce found the spot where the hogs had retreated into the bush.

"Didn't miss him by much," Wilson growled, bending to peer at the tracks. "He sure took off in a hurry."

At the campsite, Mr. Hardy frowned thoughtfully and shook his head. "He camped here more than once. This ground has been walked on quite a bit. Why, though, I wonder? What was he doing out here?"

Deputy Wilson looked curiously at Fenton Hardy. "What makes you think the man who chased these boys is the same one who made this camp?"

"Just a hunch," Mr. Hardy told him. "For one thing, the man in the mask picked Willow Creek and the lake for his trap. That means he's familiar with the area."

"Makes sense," Wilson admitted. "He could—hey, look at this." He pulled branches aside ten yards from the site of the fire. "Someone's been coming here regularly, all right. This is where he dragged his boat up to shore."

. Mr. Hardy and Professor Pierce inspected the spot, then walked back to the camp. Chet motioned Frank and Joe to his side.

"Here's something the deputy and your father missed," he said excitedly. "Look — that root sticking up through the ferns." He leaned down and came up with a piece of dried mud. "Remember the yellow mud we found behind Mr. Morgan's office—after someone tore up his place?"

Frank raised a brow. "Are you saying it came from here?"

"There are no dead termites in this piece," Chet declared, "but I'm certain it's the same mud."

"I bet he's right," Joe said tightly. "Whoever this fellow is, he used this root over and over to scrape his boots. *After* he came back from somewhere else."

Frank stared thoughtfully into the swamp. "Uh-huh. That's exactly what he did. And I'd give a lot to know just where that somewhere else is!"

Later that evening, Harrison Baker joined the others around the professor's kitchen table.

140

"Some puzzling things have been happening around here," Fenton Hardy began. "I don't have to tell any of you that. I think, though, that we now have information that can shed a little light on this case." He glanced from Pierce to Baker. "First, there's something you two should know."

Mr. Hardy explained how he and Frank had discovered that both their houses were electronically bugged. Pierce and Baker were shocked and angry. They understood, however, why they hadn't been told at the time.

"You're right," the professor admitted. "Both of us have been on edge. I'm afraid we might have given it away."

"I'm glad you understand," Mr. Hardy said. "Now, I'm going to let the boys tell you the rest of the news. They're the ones who dug it up."

Frank pulled an envelope out of his pocket and removed the two burned scraps of paper. "We found these at the campsite," he explained. "We certainly don't intend to keep this evidence from the sheriff, but we wanted you two and Dad to see it first." He looked straight at Harrison and Baker. "There are two mysteries here. One, why these papers were stolen, and two, why they were later burned out in the swamp."

Baker squinted at the scraps, then stared at the

others in disbelief. "This is incredible," he gasped. "I—I don't understand it at all!"

"Neither do we," Joe put in. "Do you recognize these papers? Do you see any reason someone might want them?"

"Oh, I recognize them, all right," Baker said at once. "The first is a fragment from a Confederate Army order. Nothing very unusual— every time an army unit moves, as you know, its headquarters issues some kind of order. I have several of these in my collection. Or I *did* have," he added bitterly, "before my study caught on fire."

"Can you tell us when and where the order was issued?" Joe asked.

"No." Baker shook his head. "I remember this particular document. The date was torn off when I got it. It could refer to any number of army movements in the Big Thicket during the war."

"And what about the piece of map we found?" Frank wanted to know.

"That's going to take a little time," Baker told him, "but I expect I can pin it down." He glanced at Fenton Hardy. "There's something I still don't understand. I would have known if anyone had been through my papers. I'm almost certain nothing was missing before my study caught on fire. And nothing was left to steal after

142

that! So how did anyone get his hands on these papers?"

Mr. Hardy cleared his throat. "I couldn't have answered that question yesterday," he said grimly. "Now, I know exactly how your documents were taken. I told the boys a few hours ago, after they showed me these scraps of paper." He paused, then faced Pierce and Baker again. "When I drove to Houston yesterday, Fire Chief Billy Wallace went with me. We took along some small, fused bits of metal the chief found at the fire and turned them over to the crime lab in Houston. That fire was no accident at all. It was started with two cleverly made incendiary devices. The sole purpose of the fire was to destroy every document in your study!"

16 Maps and Mud

Professor Pierce looked stunned. Baker doubled his fists on the table. "*Why*!" he blurted angrily. "Why would anyone want to destroy my papers? Twenty years of historical research and it's gone —material that's worthless to anyone else!"

"Someone doesn't think it's worthless," Frank said grimly. "He stole the papers and covered the theft with a fire. There has to be a reason."

"It was a professional job," Mr. Hardy said. "One incendiary device was attached to the gas pipes leading into the Armadillo Cafe. A second device was placed against the side of your house, Harrison, probably hidden behind some bushes. Both were set off seconds apart—"

"So that it looked as if the fire had spread from

144

the side of the cafe to your home," Joe finished.

"Incidentally," Fenton Hardy added, "I've asked Chief Wallace to keep this to himself. He's told no one but Sheriff Proctor, and Proctor's not going to make our findings public."

"We still don't know why those papers were taken," Pierce noted.

"No, we don't," Frank admitted. "But we have an answer to another piece of the puzzle. We know for sure we were right about the prowler who tried to force the safe in your study. It was definitely papers and maps he was after."

"Say, that's right!" Baker sat up straight and stared at Pierce. "Martin, this ought to help us narrow down what the thief was after at my house." He glanced at the others and explained. "As you know, my field is strictly history. Martin was helping me with the natural features of this area. How the land looked, how it has changed . . ."

"And we were working on one specific period," Pierce noted. "The mid-nineteenth century, and the time of the Civil War!"

"Hah! That's exactly the period our prowler is interested in," Frank said firmly. "The piece of paper he stole and burned was a Confederate Army order."

"Yes, but what order?" Baker spread his hands in dismay. "As I said, I remember the

145

document. The date was missing, and I have no idea which military action it's all about."

"I have a hunch the man who stole it could answer that," Fenton Hardy muttered.

"Right," Frank said. "Look—let's try to fit together the pieces we have. He stole an army order and a map for some reason. I think he's looking for something out in the swamp. He burned the evidence after he got the information that he needed."

Baker shook his head. "I don't know, young man. Looking for what?"

Mr. Hardy glanced to his right. "Chet, I think it's time you told them about your discovery."

"Yes, well . . ." Chet emptied two plain envelopes on the table. "I found this sample behind Mr. Morgan's office after someone had torn up the place. There are dead termites in the mud. The second sample comes from the campsite where the scraps of paper were found. The man in the mask scraped his boots on a root whenever he got out of his boat."

"It seems pretty clear that he carried that mud from somewhere else," Mr. Hardy put in. "There wasn't any of it around the site."

Pierce squinted at the dried samples, squeezed a piece between his fingers, then brought it to his nose and carefully sniffed. "It's

146

a mix of mud and clay," he said finally. "Not too uncommon, but it's only found in certain parts of the Big Thicket."

"Using the scrap of map you have," Joe said, "and knowing approximately where this guy's been taking his boat . . ."

"Yes," Pierce said, "it'll help us a great deal. With any luck, Harrison and I should be able to pin down the area where this fellow's been exploring."

"This may make sense to the rest of you," Baker muttered, "but I'm more confused than ever. What does any of this have to do with the threats on Martin's life, and this business of putting listening devices in our homes? Nelson Zeigler's after oil and timber rights in the Thicket—right now, in the twentieth century. Why does he want documents and maps from the Civil War?"

"We think Zeigler's mixed up in this," Mr. Hardy said. "We don't know for sure, though, do we?"

"*I'm* sure," Pierce said crossly. "I don't know what kind of nonsense he's up to now, but he's behind it, all right."

Joe rubbed his chin and frowned. "Would anyone have found any oil deposits around here that early?" he asked. "Could Zeigler have

147

learned something like that from your papers?"

"Definitely not," Baker said firmly. "A man named Edwin Drake sank the first well in the country that struck oil — in 1859, I believe, in northwestern Pennsylvania. No one was very excited about oil during that period. There was certainly nothing happening in the Big Thicket."

"Well, there's something out there," Frank sighed. "That character in the ski mask isn't playing games."

"Martin and I will put our heads together right now," Harrison Baker assured him. "We'll let you know the moment we come up with anything at all."

"Good," Frank said. "The sooner the better."

At that moment, someone stepped onto the front porch and knocked on the door. Chet walked into the hall and called over his shoulder. "It's Deputy Wilson. And Mr. Fields is with him."

Fenton Hardy looked quickly at the others. "For the time being, let's keep all of this to ourselves. I'd like some solid answers before we say too much."

Everyone nodded in agreement. Chet went down the hall to let Wilson and Fields inside. The tall deputy's eyes swept the room.

"Well," he said, "I can tell right off you haven't heard the latest news."

"What news?" Joe asked eagerly.

"It happened not ten minutes ago," Wilson went on. "Rake Morgan caught Nelson Zeigler coming out of the Lansdale Hotel and accused the guy of tearing up his office, and trying to ambush you fellows at Moccasin Point. Zeigler knocked Morgan down, got in his car and chased Morgan around the square. Drove right across the courthouse lawn and nearly caught him. Missed running him down by a couple of inches. Zeigler took off, and the sheriff took after him."

"Wow," Chet said, "there's never a dull moment in this town!"

"I'd just as soon it'd go back to bein' dull," Wilson said dryly.

"So now what?" Frank asked. "What's going to happen when Sheriff Proctor catches up with Mr. Zeigler?"

"He'll go to jail, I imagine," Wilson said flatly. "Rake Morgan's already said he'll press charges against Zeigler for trying to run him down. And you can bet he'll do it, too."

"Mr. Fields," Joe asked curiously, "do you still think your former employer's not involved in the things that have been happening here?"

149

"I don't know what to think," Fields said wearily. "He tried to run down Rake Morgan. I don't know for certain he's done anything else."

"Huh!" Pierce said sourly. "You're entitled to your opinion."

Mr. Baker and the professor have some work to finish up," Frank spoke up. "Maybe we could talk out on the porch."

"I'll join you later," Mr. Hardy said. "First I have a couple of phone calls to make."

When the group had assembled outside, a glint of excitement came into Turner Fields' eyes. "We have something to show you," he said to the Hardys. "Right, Deputy Wilson?"

"This is all your idea, Mr. Fields," Wilson said. "I reckon you ought to tell 'em."

"Tell us what?" Joe asked.

Fields took a hand-drawn map out of his jacket and spread it across his knees. "I've been interested in this 'monster alligator' mystery," he confessed. "You know—collecting the newspaper stories on the sightings, talking to people who've actually seen the thing. Like you three," he added with a grin. "Anyway, I started charting the sightings and, uh—I came up with this. I'm not sure it means anything at all."

"Makes a lot of sense to me," Wilson said solemnly.

"Here," Fields pointed, "these are the spots in the Thicket where the alligator has been seen. The last sighting, by the way, was early this morning. Did you hear about that?"

Frank, Joe and Chet looked at each other and frowned. "No, we didn't hear a thing," Frank said. "What happened?"

"Didn't think you knew," Fields nodded. "From what Deputy Wilson here says, you were plenty busy about that time with problems of your own. It happened right here—" He stabbed the chart with his finger. "Scared the daylights out of some tourists. Anyway . . . take a look at the pattern of these sightings. There are nine of them in all now. Do you notice anything peculiar?"

Frank, Joe and Chet studied the chart. "Hey," Joe said suddenly, "the dots you've drawn form some kind of a circle—or a lop-sided square!"

"Right," Fields said. "Now, if we connect these dots . . ." He paused, and laid a second piece of paper over the first. "See? The center of our figure is roughly—there."

"I see where you're going with this," Frank said thoughtfully. "If that creature was spotted in these different locations, he just might live somewhere right in the middle."

"It's possible," Fields said. "I don't know

151

much about alligators, but from what I understand, they're pretty territorial in nature. They pick out an area all their own and then stick pretty close to home."

"What Mr. Fields has in mind," Deputy Wilson explained, "is to take a good look at that area in the center of the circle. We thought maybe you boys would like to come along!"

17   The Trap

It was dark when Deputy Wilson pulled his four-wheel-drive car to a halt on the narrow dirt road. Frank, Joe and Chet gathered around the lawman and Turner Fields by a large oak. Fields pointed a small penlight at his map.

"Okay," he said quietly, "if my calculations are right, the alligator's home ground should center around Blue Hollow Swamp. We've covered the creeks leading out of that area from the south and the west. He could be in those sections, but according to you, Bob, that isn't very likely, right?"

"I don't think so," Deputy Wilson said. "A creature that size has a mighty big appetite. If he'd been anywhere close to the spots we've covered, every living thing would have cleared out by now and he'd have the place to himself. Yet there's plenty of game left in those areas."

"Which means I'm either wrong," Fields said wryly, "or he might be in the section we're in right now. Here, on Little Frog Branch. Or here," he pointed, "just north of this road, on Black Bear Bayou."

"I'd say the bayou's a bad bet," Wilson advised. "Too open. Not enough cover."

"Then let's try Little Frog," Frank suggested. "According to the map, it shouldn't be very far."

"The creek goes right past the bend up ahead," Wilson told him.

Fields glanced at his watch. "It's close to sundown. We'd better take it slow, and make as little noise as we can."

"Stay away from the water," Wilson warned them. "We don't know what time this thing eats his supper. . . ."

Chet stared at the lawman. "Did you—have to remind us of that?"

"Just keep your eyes open, son," Wilson smiled.

Frank and Chet took the upper branch of the creek with Deputy Wilson, while Joe joined

Turner Fields downstream. The ancient, thick-trunked oaks were bearded with Spanish moss. The ground was a carpet of broad-leafed ferns.

"This cover helps," Fields whispered. "We can see clear across the creek, and nothing out there can see us."

"That's good news," Joe said soberly. He walked behind Fields, bending now and then beneath gray veils of moss. The light was fading fast. An owl streaked low, looking for careless mice. Suddenly, Joe heard something move in the water. He stopped in his tracks and aimed his large flashlight at the creek.

"Hold it," Fields cautioned, grasping Joe's arm. "Don't turn the light on yet. I saw it—it was only a fish."

"Okay," Joe said and walked on silently, following in Turner Fields' path. The creek flowed south, then gradually swung to the west. Joe tried to recall Fields' map. If he remembered it correctly, the creek narrowed soon and disappeared into the swamp. Another few yards and they would have to turn around and go back.

Fields seemed to guess his thoughts. "This is about it," he said quietly. "Let's follow the same plan we've used before. On the way back, you search the far bank with your light, and I'll see what I can spot on this side." .

"Right," Joe agreed. "Maybe we'll have a little luck this time and—"

Fields suddenly motioned him to silence. "Hey, did you hear that?"

Joe listened. "No, I don't hear a thing."

Fields frowned in thought. "Come on, it's worth a look."

He made his way stealthily through the trees. Joe crept along behind. Suddenly, Fields stopped abruptly and stood up straight.

"Wh—what on earth—!" he exclaimed. "Joe, look at this!" He moved aside and motioned the boy over. The two stared curiously at the sight. There was a van parked ten yards away, nearly concealed behind low hanging moss! The paint was so rusted and weathered, it was hard to tell in the dark what color it had been. Behind the van was a boat trailer covered in patched canvas.

Joe and Turner Fields could make out the dim peaks of two camping tents. The tents were made of camouflage print, common in army-navy surplus stores.

"Who do you suppose this belongs to?" the young detective whispered to Fields. "Who'd want to camp out here?"

"I don't know," Fields said. "I thought the

place was abandoned, but I did hear something. If someone's around, I don't want to scare him to death." Fields cleared his throat and flicked his light on the ground at his feet. "Hello, is anyone here?" he called out cautiously. "Anyone home?"

Suddenly, the flap on one of the tents flew open. Joe brought up his light and caught a pale, startled face in the beam.

"Hawks," Joe exclaimed under his breath, "it's—*Lew Hawks!*"

Hawks stared, blinded by the light. He yelled over his shoulder, bolted from the tent and vanished into the dark. Joe saw another figure right on his heels and knew it was Shiner Black.

"Those two are up to something," Joe blurted. "I know it!"

"Wilson!" Fields cupped his hands and shouted. "Stop those two coming your way! "We'll head 'em off from behind."

Moments later, lights flashed through the bearded moss. Shouts of anger reached Joe's ears, then Lew and Shiner appeared, walking sullenly ahead of Deputy Wilson.

"I don't know what you're doing out here," Wilson growled, "but I bet it's something I'm not going to like."

157

Hawks and Black glared at Joe, then Wilson herded them back to their camp. Frank and Chet looked on curiously.

"What's this all about?" Frank asked.

"Beats me," Joe told him. "We were searching for giant alligators and found these two instead."

"I think I like the alligator better," Chet said darkly.

"You just take it real easy," Wilson told the pair. He leaned into the van and poked his light around in the dark. Then he walked behind the van and inspected the canvas-covered trailer. "Now let me guess what you've got under here," he said wryly. "Wouldn't be somebody's shiny new boat you stole, would it?" Wilson loosened the canvas straps and threw them aside. "We'll just take a look an—" Wilson stopped, dropped the canvas and stumbled back. "Now what kind of boat would you call that?" he exclaimed.

"Leaping lizards!" Joe blurted.

Everyone pointed their light beams at the hideous creation on the trailer. It was a giant alligator, fifteen feet long from tail to ugly snout. Its jaws were clamped shut, but the boys could see long rows of sharp, ivory-colored teeth.

Frank walked carefully up to the monster and touched its warty hide. "It's some kind of rubber or plastic," he said in wonder. "It's a fake, but it's the best fake I ever saw."

"Take a look at this," Joe said. He walked from one of the tents holding a black metal box no larger than an average-sized book. There were several switches and dials on top. "It's a radio control device," he announced. "That's how they did it! I'll bet you can make this thing do anything you want. Go forward, backward, under water . . ."

"And don't forget the working of the jaws," Chet added.

Frank turned to Deputy Wilson. "This thing isn't any toy—it's full of expensive electronics. Whoever had it made must have spent a bundle."

"No question about that," Wilson agreed. He looked at Hawks and Black. "And it wasn't you two, was it? Come on, let's have it. You have a lot of explaining to do!"

Shiner Black was frightened, but Lew Hawks glared defiantly at Wilson. "We don't have a thing to say to you," he snapped. "Nothing!"

"Suits me," Wilson shrugged. "You fellows want to take all the trouble that's coming your way, that's your business."

"Hey, w—wait a minute!" Shiner blurted.

"Shut up!" Lew growled.

Black stared at his friend. "Are you crazy? You think he's going to protect us!"

"Who?" Wilson demanded. "Who are you talking about?"

Lew bit his lip and looked at the ground. "All right," he muttered. "This guy hired us to do it. He—he said it was just a joke, but we aren't that stupid. It wasn't any joke."

"Get on with it," Wilson said tightly. "Who's behind all this?"

Lew's shoulders sagged. "It was—Mr. Zeigler. Nelson Zeigler. The rich guy."

18   *Questions and Answers*

"*What!*" Turner Fields shook his head in disbelief. "Wilson, these two are lying. Nelson Zeigler would never pull a stunt like this!"

"You think whatever you want, mister," Shiner Black said angrily. "It was him, all right!"

"Why?" Joe asked. "You said just now that you knew it was more than a joke. Zeigler never told you what the monster was for, did he?"

"He didn't have to," Lew said haughtily. He sneered at Joe and leaned against the van. "I figured it out for myself. I know what's going on in this town—all the trouble between Professor Pierce and Zeigler. The monster was to get people worried—tourists, and people who live here, too. He wanted everyone to think the Big Thicket was a dangerous place to be. Full of— giant alligators and stuff. He had other ideas, too. He asked me once what I thought about wearing a scary suit. Some kinda swamp creature, like in the movies." Lew laughed bitterly. "He said it'd be a swell joke, but I knew what he was doing."

"And after all that," Joe said darkly, "maybe the public wouldn't care about preserving the natural beauty of this place. No one would bother to stop Zeigler from taking all the oil and timber he wanted."

Deputy Wilson wiped a bandanna across his face. "All right," he said wearily, "let's get you two and your monster back to town. I can't wait till Vard Proctor sees this contraption."

"I'll get even with you guys," Lew Hawks shouted, shaking his fist at the three friends. "You wait and see if I don't!"

"If I were you," Wilson said flatly, "I'd be a lot more worried about getting out than getting even!"

Half an hour later, the deputy parked in front of the sheriff's office and took his two prisoners inside. Soon, Frank arrived in the rusty van, towing the captured 'monster' behind. Word spread quickly, and the town square was soon filled with people. Even resting motionless on its trailer, the giant alligator was a frightening sight to see.

Rake Morgan walked out of the sheriff's office and stared in wonder. "I can't believe it," he exclaimed. "I never saw anything like that in my life!"

"Wilson has the pair that ran this thing," Turner Fields explained. "We caught them red-handed and they confessed."

"Lew Hawks and Shiner Black? I saw Wilson bringing them in. They're responsible for this?"

"They operated the monster," Joe told him, "but Nelson Zeigler's behind it."

"Hah!" Morgan crowed. "I'm not at all surprised." He grinned and nodded over his shoulder. "I guess this is a good night for catching criminals. Zeigler himself is in there right now, too. Proctor caught up with him and brought him back. He's already been charged with trying to run me down. Now Vard's questioning him about all the other stuff that's been happening around here." He glanced at the monster and shook his head. "I think I'll go back inside. I can't wait to hear what Zeigler says when he finds out they've caught Hawks and Black."

"I'll come with you," Fields sighed.

"Congratulations, boys," Morgan boomed. "You did a great job!"

Morgan and Fields walked away. Frank watched them disappear, then turned to Joe and Chet. "I don't think Mr. Fields is real happy about Lew and Shiner being caught," he said.

"I know he's not," Joe replied. "He still doesn't want to believe Zeigler's mixed up in this."

"He'll have to get used to it," Chet put in. "His former boss is up to his neck in trouble. Oh, hey—there's your dad."

Frank and Joe saw Mr. Hardy leave the sheriff's office and work his way through the crowd. He looked at the giant alligator and frowned. "Looks like you boys have had a busy night," he said evenly. "Fields told me what happened, but I want to hear all about it from you three."

"Is there any news on Mr. Zeigler?" Frank asked.

"No, except he swears he's had nothing to do with threatening Professor Pierce, and that he wasn't involved in setting that fire. Come on, let's get out of here and go back to the house." His mouth curved in a knowing grin. "That's where the real news may be waiting. Pierce and

Baker have come up with some interesting answers."

"What?" Joe asked eagerly. "I know that look of yours, Dad. Something's going on!"

"Maybe, and maybe not," Mr. Hardy winked at his son. "We'll see what you can make of their findings."

When they arrived at the professor's, the boys were disappointed to find Pierce and Baker still busy at work. They were locked in the dining room, poring over stacks of books. They promised to come out soon, but refused to give a hint of what they were doing.

Mr. Hardy settled back in a chair. "Now, it's time you fellows told *me* a little news. Honestly, I never imagined this idea of Turner Fields' would get results. Tell me everything that has happened."

Frank recounted their capture of Hawks and Black, and their discovery of the giant alligator.

"I haven't had a chance to examine that thing closely," Mr. Hardy said thoughtfully when his son was finished. "But you boys are right — a contraption like that would cost a small fortune to build. I wonder where Zeigler would—"

"Dad," Frank interrupted, coming halfway out

165

of his chair, "I think I might know the answer to that one. You showed us a list, once, of the different companies owned by the Zeigco Corporation."

"Why, yes, I did," Mr. Hardy replied.

"Mount Olympus Productions," Frank went on, "and Zeigler Electronics."

"I know what you're thinking," Fenton Hardy said. "Don't forget Hokkaido Laboratories and Aegean Computers."

"A motion picture studio, electronics firms, computers," Frank finished. "A man like Zeigler could have a machine like that alligator built anywhere in the world. He has the money and the expertise right at his fingertips."

"If he did," Joe added, "the police will eventually find out where the work was done. An awful lot of people would be involved in a project like that."

Fenton Hardy scratched his chin. "You've hit the nail right on the head, Joe. If Zeigler used his own companies to build that creature, I'm afraid he made a serious mistake."

There was a knock at the door, and Sheriff Proctor came in. He took off his hat and let out a breath. "We're about finished for the night, and I wanted to stop by and let you folks know where we stand. We didn't get a thing out of

Zeigler. Didn't expect to, really. He was hopping mad when I confronted him with the confessions of Hawks and Black. Turned red in the face and swore those two were lying."

"You're still holding him, aren't you?" Joe asked.

Sheriff Proctor frowned. "I'm charging him, of course, but we're not holding him any more. He had four lawyers up here from Houston quicker than you can whistle. He's out on bail right now. Took off in a hurry out of town."

"I'm not surprised," Mr. Hardy said.

"We got some interesting facts out of Lew and Shiner," Proctor went on. "They only met Zeigler twice, both times at night south of town. It was pitch dark, but they identified Zeigler and that big car of his. The rest of the time, he gave them instructions by phone — where and when to have that alligator appear. He was supposed to meet them tonight. That's why they were waiting at the spot where they kept the van and the trailer."

"What about the other incidents?" Joe asked. "Did they confess to those?"

"Not a one." Proctor made a face. "I don't say I believe 'em, but they swear all they did was operate that alligator for Zeigler. They deny they stampeded those horses, and say they weren't the pair in the boat when that woodpecker got blasted into feathers. They claim that they had nothing to do with setting fire to the cafe and Baker's house, and that they haven't sent any threatening letters."

"They could be telling the truth," Frank said. "There's the prowler who broke into the professor's study, and the man in the ski mask who tried to carry off Marilyn Baker. And that was probably the same guy who chased us out in the swamp."

"Don't forget that coral snake," Chet reminded him. "And the man in the truck who tried to run us off the road. And someone broke into Mr. Morgan's office."

"I know Lew and Shiner didn't put that alligator in Martin's car way up in Bayport," Mr. Hardy said.

"Right," Proctor muttered under his breath. "Zeigler himself has to be responsible for some of the things that have been happening. And we don't know who else he has working for him." The sheriff replaced his hat on his head. "We'll find out," he said evenly. "Whoever's involved will be spending time in jail with Nelson Zeigler before this is over."

He stood up and said goodnight, and Joe saw him to the door.

"Someone else has to be mixed up in this business," Frank said. "Mr. Zeigler wouldn't trust Hawks and Black alone to handle something like that fire—or breaking into the professor's study."

"He made a big mistake trusting them at all," Joe said. "Look how fast they talked when they got caught!"

Frank shook his head. "There's something wrong with that. Mr. Zeigler's not that dumb."

"No, he's not," Mr. Hardy agreed.

"Look," Joe said, "all along we've been figuring that—"

He stopped as Pierce opened the door to the dining room. "All right," he said wearily, "if you'll all join us, we'll tell you what we have so far."

"That's what we've been waiting for," Joe exclaimed. "You don't have to ask us twice!"

Everyone crowded around the table. Baker shoved their work aside to make room.

"First," Pierce began, "we don't have the solution to this puzzle, but we have come up with some answers that may help."

He spread his map on the table. "Here's the lake and Moccasin Point," he explained, "and the spot where the campfire was found. And here, about six miles east . . ." He paused and grinned at Chet, ". . . is the place where we think your yellow mud comes from. It's a pretty dense section of Shadow Marsh with lots of baygalls and thickets that no one would care to cross."

"Unless they were looking for something they wanted real bad," Joe muttered.

"Exactly," Baker put in. "And that's what we've been trying to figure out. All of my papers were lost in the fire, but I've gathered up some good reference works, and my memory's pretty sound. I think this is the place your masked friend is eager to explore. So, the next logical step is to connect this area with some action in the Civil War." He paused, and let his gaze touch everyone in the room. "There was only one incident that took place anywhere near this spot. . . ."

"W—wait a minute!" Frank stood up and stared at the map. "Now I remember. You showed us this spot on the map once before!"

"You're right," Baker said solemnly, "I did. Somewhere in that area is the place where the Lost Column disappeared!"

19 The Culprit

Joe shook his head and stared. "The more we find out about this case, the more puzzling it gets! Zeigler threatens the professor, hires two bullies to run his fake alligator, someone sets fire to Mr. Baker's study—"

"And now we've got this Lost Column business," Chet finished. "I don't get it. The Civil War's been over more than a hundred years."

"There's something funny going on out in the swamp," Fenton Hardy said solemnly. "And somehow it's mixed up with what's happening right here in Black Cypress Creek."

"I guess I know more about the Lost Column than anyone," Baker said. "I've studied the incident for years, mostly because of our celebration. There's just *not* that much to know. The Jayhawkers attacked a Confederate supply column. The Rebels were beaten, and the wagons sank into the swamp. Most writers give it a sentence or two in Civil War histories—if they mention it at all."

"Maybe we're all wet," Pierce said. "Could you have, ah—made a mistake, Harrison?"

Baker laughed. "I make mistakes all the time. But I didn't make one on this. That action definitely took place somewhere in the area shown on that burned scrap of map the boys found."

"You haven't mentioned the other piece of paper," Joe said. "The fragment of a Confederate army order."

"I know what you're thinking," Baker said. "You found the order and the map in one place, so you think they go together. Maybe they do. Maybe those shipment numbers—what was it? Yes, 7110 and 7111—Maybe they refer to items in the Lost Column supply train. But we can't prove it."

"Sir, just suppose someone found a piece to the Lost Column puzzle that no one knows about," Joe suggested. "That would explain why things have been happening around here, wouldn't it?"

Harrison Baker frowned. "I'm not sure I understand."

"I think I do," Frank said. "We don't see any connection between Zeigler wanting oil and timber rights and a minor Civil War battle. Now, it looks as if the Lost Column has been a part of this case all along. Someone's gone to a lot of trouble to keep us looking in *this* century instead of the one before."

"Nonsense," Pierce snapped. "Are you saying Zeigler isn't after those rights? That's ridiculous!"

"Sir, I don't think Frank's saying that at all," Joe put in. "But there's something else here, too. Dad, remember what you said when you first arrived? That for a man who's gone as far as he has in the world, Nelson Zeigler wasn't acting very smart?"

"Yes," Mr. Hardy recalled. "He isn't acting smart if he's guilty. Or, he's acting a lot smarter than we think."

"I get it," Chet said. "He's making us think he's guilty of one crime while he's really guilty of another?"

"Remember, Chet," Frank said, "Nelson Zeigler's been accused—he hasn't been convicted."

"He will be," Pierce said tightly. "You can bet

173

on it, young man!"

"I'll go along with that," Baker agreed, "but I'm afraid Joe's right. A vital piece in the Lost Column puzzle is missing. Unless Zeigler or someone who's working with him makes a full confession, we may never know the answer to this mystery."

"We're forgetting one thing," Joe said. His face suddenly creased in a broad grin. "Whoever's behind all this doesn't know just how close we've come to uncovering his secret."

Frank's smile matched his brother's. "Now you're talking. He doesn't have any idea how much we've found out about his scheme. Maybe we can figure out some way to help him."

Pierce looked puzzled. "What are you talking about? Why on earth would we want to do that?"

Fenton Hardy's eyes gleamed in approval. "Joe, why don't you, Frank and Chet go upstairs and have a little talk? I have a good idea what you're up to, and it might just give us the answers we need!"

Half an hour later, the group gathered again around the table. Joe explained their plan, and when everyone was certain they knew exactly what to do, Joe led them into Professor Pierce's study. At a silent signal from Frank, Pierce began to speak.

"I don't know," he said, letting concern color his voice, "I'd feel a lot better if we turned this over to Vard Proctor right now."

"Martin," Fenton Hardy said, "if I was at all worried, I'd drive it down there myself. Besides, it's nearly midnight—Proctor's probably gone to bed."

"Dad's right, professor," Joe said. "Anyway, no one knows we even *have* this thing. How are they going to find out?"

"I'm afraid I agree with Martin," Baker said harshly. "Fenton, the evidence in that jar is going to blow this mystery wide open. Someone who thinks he's made fools of us is going to spend a long time in jail as soon as we hand that over to the law."

"And we will," Mr. Hardy said calmly. "Right now, though, I think we should quit worrying and get some sleep. Chet—just leave the jar in here on the professor's desk. It's not going anywhere until morning."

"Have it your way, then," Baker said curtly. "I'm going home. I can see there's no way to talk any sense into you people."

Baker stamped out of the study. A moment later, they heard him slam the front door.

"Boy, he sure was mad," Frank said. "Dad —maybe he's right. Maybe we *should* take this to the sheriff right now."

"Don't you start being silly, too," Fenton Hardy yawned. "Just go to bed and get some rest. Turn out the light, Chet."

Chet did as he was told. They left the study and went upstairs to their rooms. A few minutes later, lights winked out all over the house.

Frank, Chet and Joe sat quietly on their beds. They had changed their clothes quickly, and now wore dark trousers and T-shirts.

"All right," Frank said softly, "let's go."

The three boys walked into the hall, each carrying a flashlight. At the top of the stairs, they stopped and waited. A door opened softly nearby, and then another. Two dark shadows came toward them, Fenton Hardy and Pierce. Together, they made their way to the bottom of the stairs. Without exchanging a word, everyone moved to his assigned position. Mr. Hardy and Chet crouched on the floor outside the study. Professor Pierce took up his post near a living room window. Joe and Frank crept out the back door, to the corner of the house and hid in the shadow of the trees. From there, they could clearly see the outside window of Pierce's study.

"This had better work," Frank whispered. "If it doesn't, we're going to spend a long night outdoors."

"It'll work," Joe assured him, "if our mystery

man still has the professor's study bugged. He can't afford *not* to show up, because he has to find out what we've got."

For a long time, neither of the two spoke. There was a half-moon in the sky, masked by fleeting clouds. A warm breeze rustled the leaves overhead. Frank glanced at the luminous face of his watch. Only 12:48. He was surprised they hadn't been there longer. Maybe Joe's idea wouldn't work. Maybe the man in the mask wasn't listening to his recorder any more—

Joe's fingers clamped tightly on his shoulder. Frank started, then peered in the direction of Joe's nod. At first he saw nothing at all, only the same dark patches through the trees. Then, suddenly, one of the shadows began to move. Frank's heart pounded against his chest. A man slid silently from one tree to the next. Frank knew he was waiting, searching for sights and sounds. Finally, he crept stealthily across the stretch of open ground to the side of the house. He moved up to the window of the study, detached the screen, and then slowly raised the window. Without a sound, he climbed over the sill and disappeared inside.

"He took the bait!" Joe whispered.

Frank didn't answer. In a moment, the shadow appeared again and slid to the ground. Frank waited until the prowler reached up to replace the screen, then grasped his brother's arm and came to his feet.

"Okay," he snapped, "let's get him!"

The pair came out of the trees, moving close to the ground toward the intruder. The man whirled around and saw them. He dropped the screen and ran. Joe leaped through the air in a flying tackle. The suspect yelled and went down hard. Something flew out of his jacket and shattered on the ground. He got to his feet and lashed out at Joe with a big fist. But Joe ducked, and Frank hit the man with a good lineman's block. The intruder stumbled back, rolled on the grass and came to his feet. He started to run, then stopped. He let out a frightening bellow and tore frantically at his clothes.

Joe stepped back and clicked on his flashlight, while Frank ripped the black ski mask from the suspect's face. The man shrank back, glared angrily at Frank and shielded his eyes against the light.

"Fields!" Joe cried out. *"Turner Fields!"*

"Something's all over me," Fields screamed, slapping at his clothing. "Get—these—things—off me!"

"I guess you broke your evidence," Frank

grinned. "That was Chet's idea—to fill the jar with ants."

"Get 'em off me," Fields shrieked. "Hurry!"

"Hold it right there," came a voice from the darkness.

Frank and Joe turned to see Deputy Bob Wilson step quickly around the corner of the house. Mr. Hardy, Professor Pierce and Chet were right behind him. Fields snarled in anger as Wilson snapped handcuffs around his wrists.

"You've got a lot of questions to answer, fellow," Wilson told him.

"I'm just following orders," Fields snapped angrily. "Zeigler's the one you want!"

"Huh-uh, I don't think so," Frank said.

"You'll never prove a thing against me!" Fields blurted.

"Maybe this gentleman will give us some help . . ."

Frank, Joe and the others turned to see Sheriff Proctor leading Rake Morgan through the trees. Harrison Baker was following them, holding a flashlight.

"I don't know what you think you're doing," Morgan said tightly. "Let go of me this instant or you're in serious trouble, sheriff! I was just— sitting in my car. There's no law against that!"

Proctor let out a sigh. "I'm sorry, Mr. Morgan. I was already there when you drove up. I saw who was in the car with you, and who got out and sneaked up to Professor Pierce's house. It was Turner Fields."

Proctor grinned at Frank and Joe. "I guess you boys caught *two* snakes in your trap instead of one."

20   Secrets Revealed

Marilyn, Bea and E.D. drove the boys down a winding dirt road to Rock Creek. The water was blue and clear, a natural swimming hole carved out of the stony bank.

"Hey, there's even a rope swing," Chet exclaimed. "I can show you my famous Tarzan act!"

Frank and Joe groaned and the girls laughed. The boys carried picnic baskets out of the Jeep and then lost no time in getting into the water. The girls shrieked and joined them. Later, when everyone had had a refreshing swim, they rested on a ledge over the pool.

"I'm glad you fellows could all stay a few

more days," Marilyn grinned. "I think you de-serve a vacation."

"It'll be pleasant without giant alligators and masked men," Frank said.

"I'm still a little confused," Marilyn admitted. "I don't understand how Turner Fields got away with what he did."

"And Rake Morgan," Bea put in. "I always liked him, too—and I couldn't stand Mr. Zeigler. He's such an old sourpuss!"

"Zeigler's not very likable and his bad temper's famous all over the world," Joe said. "Fields counted on that. He knew his boss would make himself look guilty—if Fields just gave him a little help."

"Then it's true what they're saying?" Bea asked. "Mr. Zeigler didn't do anything at all?"

He tried to run Morgan down—after Morgan deliberately pushed him too far. But that's all he did."

"Turner Fields set him up from the start," Frank added. "He did a pretty good job of it, too."

"And everyone in town thought it was Zeigler who was threatening the professor—trying to get those oil and timber rights for his company!" E.D. shook her head in wonder.

"Oh, Zeigler wanted those rights," Frank said. "Fields hid behind that business to get what *he* was really after."

"The secret of the Lost Column, right?" Marilyn said. "That's what it was all about."

"That's it," Joe told her. "It all came out in Fields' confession. Nearly a year ago, he was in charge of a crew of Zeigco experts looking over the Thicket. He found the remains of an old cabin back in the swamp. Most of it was eaten up by rot and bugs. That's where Chet's famous termites and yellow mud came from."

"Right," Chet yawned. "Just a little *expert* detective work is all we needed to figure that out."

Joe grinned. "It was good detective work, Chet. Anyway, Fields found a leather map case in the ruins. It fell apart when he opened it up, but there was an oilskin packet inside, still partially watertight after more than a hundred years. Inside were some personal letters to a Confederate officer—and some faded orders for his unit."

"Here's where the case gets interesting," Frank broke in. "One sheet was a list of supplies—blankets, flour, gunpowder, things like that. But there was another sheet, too, a page marked SECRET. All it said was: *Item*

7115: Gold shipment: 3,000 oz.

"Wow!" E.D. said. "So that's what Turner Fields was after!"

"Yes, but not until later," Frank told her. "At the time, he just thought he'd found an interesting souvenir. Then, he started hearing about the Jayhawkers and Rebels' celebration. He met your father, Marilyn, and learned a little about the history of the Lost Column. He suddenly realized what his souvenir might mean. The column was attacked somewhere in the area where he'd found that packet. If the Confederate officer who'd left his map case in that cabin was with the Lost Column—"

"Then that gold might still be in one of the wagons that sank in the swamp!" Marilyn finished.

"Right. And since the orders concerning the gold shipment were 'secret,' no one else in the world knew any gold was with the column!"

"And remember," Joe put in, "3,000 ounces of gold was worth over $100,000 in the 1860s. It's worth ten times that much now."

"Wow," Bea gasped. "A—a *million dollars buried in the swamp!*"

"Fields needed help from someone who lived around here," Frank continued. "He learned a little about Morgan and found he'd pulled some

184

shady deals in the past. He approached Morgan, who couldn't resist the idea of a million in gold.

"To get it, they had to know exactly where it was. And they had to keep people away from the site. If Zeigco brought men and machines into the swamp, Fields would never be able to salvage the gold. So, he had to ruin negotiations between Zeigler and Pierce."

"Right," Joe added. "It was Fields who flew up secretly to Bayport and put that alligator in Pierce's car. He and Morgan sent all the threatening notes, too. They say they only meant to scare Pierce, that they never intended to harm him. Maybe they did and maybe they didn't. It was Fields who tried to run us off the road when we arrived. And he tossed the coral snake into your father's house, Marilyn."

"And all the time he was pretending to be our friend," Marilyn said, "and saying he was sure Zeigler was innocent."

"Why did he break into the professor's study?" E.D. asked.

"He kept talking to Mr. Baker," Joe said, "trying to learn where the gold might be without making Baker suspicious. He didn't want to break into Baker's study unless he had to. He knew Pierce and Baker had worked together, so he tried the professor's house first."

"I'm puzzled about something else," Bea said. "How did they manage to shoot that ivory-billed woodpecker? You all saw it explode when they shot it!"

"It exploded, all right," Frank said grimly. "But the bird wasn't alive. It was a stuffed specimen Fields had stolen from a museum. Of course, it was Fields and Morgan in the boat— and they deliberately wore Zeigco patches so Zeigler would get the blame. The trick worked. Pierce would have nothing to do with Zeigler after that."

"And Fields stampeded those horses at the Jayhawkers and Rebels' battle?" E.D. asked.

"Right," Joe answered. "As you've probably guessed, Morgan wrecked his own office and blamed it on Zeigler. The mud Chet found that night was left by Fields, coming back from one of his expeditions in the swamp."

"Who tried to carry me off after I surprised him in the yard?" Marilyn asked. "Was that Fields or Morgan?"

"That was Morgan," Frank said. "He planted the listening devices at your house, and at the professor's."

"Fields was getting desperate for more information," Joe said. "We knew about the bugs, so we weren't saying anything he and Morgan could use. Fields decided he had to try to pin

186

down the location of the Lost Column. Baker couldn't pinpoint the spot — nobody was sure where the wagons disappeared. But, knowing what he knew already, Fields thought he could find what he needed in Baker's papers."

"So he set those incendiary devices," Marilyn said, "went through Dad's papers, and then met him in front of the cafe."

"It was a clever plan," Frank had to admit. "He was sitting with your dad in the Armadillo Cafe when Morgan set off the devices from a distance. He even became a hero by rushing into your dad's house and stopping him from going into his burning study."

"Some hero," Bea said darkly.

"He had to set the fire to cover up the fact that he had broken in," Frank went on. "He got what he wanted, too. A better map of the area and a set of old orders. Remember? The scrap he burned referred to shipments 7110 and 7111. When he found that, Fields knew he was on the right track. His gold shipment number was 7115. Mr. Baker had one of the orders from the Lost Column and didn't know it. Not then, anyway. Fields, though, was certain he had the right spot, since the sequence of numbers matched."

"Fields made a big mistake luring us out to Moccasin Point," Joe said. "I can't prove it, but I don't think he merely intended to scare us. If

187

he hadn't picked an area he knew well, we wouldn't have found those scraps he tried to burn. And they were a big help in cracking the case."

"Meanwhile, Rake Morgan kept pushing Zeigler into losing his temper," Bea said. "He got Zeigler mad enough to try to run him down."

"Exactly," Frank said. "And everything Fields and Morgan did made Zeigler look a lot worse."

"Like that fake alligator," Joe said.

"I'm still wondering about that," E.D. said. "I thought Hawks and Black identified Zeigler as the man who hired them."

"They did. But it was really Turner Fields, using Zeigler's car. Remember—Hawks and Black only met him twice, on a dark night. They couldn't see his face clearly, they only assumed it was Zeigler because Fields told them that's who he was. He has known Zeigler for years, and probably did a good-enough imitation of his boss's voice."

"And then Fields cleverly led us to the spot where Hawks and Black kept the fake alligator," Joe added. "It wasn't hard, since he knew right where it was, and had told Hawks and Black to be there."

"And poor Mr. Zeigler got the blame again," Bea sighed.

"Sure," Joe said. "Fields meant to let Hawks

and Black get caught eventually. "It wasn't hard for him to have the monster built secretly at Zeigco. The people involved thought their orders were coming from Zeigler himself. And the 'capture' of the monster worked out fine for Fields and Morgan. Deputy Wilson brought in Hawks and Black at the same time Proctor captured Zeigler."

"We knew from the start it was odd that everything that happened looked as if Zeigler was behind it," Frank said. "And when those Lost Column clues turned up . . ."

"Do you think they'll ever find all that gold?" E.D. asked. "Do you suppose it's really there?"

"I think it's there," Joe said.

"Talking about those clues to the Lost Column gave you a chance to use the listening device Morgan had planted at the professor's house to trap the culprits," E.D. said. "That was a great scheme!"

"You'll have to admit," Chet spoke up, "my ants played a big part in solving this case."

"We'll make a deal with you," Joe grinned. "You get credit for solving the case, and we get a chance at those barbecued ribs and fried chicken before you do."

"Huh?" Chet's face fell. "What kind of deal is that?"

Everyone laughed, and the young people continued to tease Chet about his appetite. Only Frank did not participate in the banter. He was wondering if the Hardys would ever get another mystery like this one to work on. Somehow he knew that they would!